Withered Pages

Dragonfire Press
FLAME

Cover design by Keith Robinson

Dragonfire Press Flame is an imprint of Dragonfire Press

e-Book ISBN: 978-1-958354-36-0

Print ISBN: 978-1-958354-37-7

Withered Pages

Amanda Guerrero-Porter

OTHER BOOKS

The Witches of Thyana

Songs of Ruin
The Sacrifice of Ava Black
The Second Death of Ava Black

The Darkness Trilogy

The Shadow
The Forsaken
The Redeemed

Anthologies

Magic of Mirstone
Quests of Mirstone
Endless Moonlight

Other Works

Pieces of My Heart
Pieces of My Soul
Nexus Dimensions

Author's Note

Dear Reader,

I would like to give you the opportunity to read this book with a clear understanding of what you are getting yourself into. While this book is fiction, there are very real themes reflected in my work. There is mention of SA, but there are no details or explicit words regarding it. It is something that causes a character trauma, however. There is loss of life mentioned due to violence and tragic accidents. Lastly, there is loss of life regarding an animal. All these themes are never written explicitly. Again, I wanted you to know these things before you made the decision to read further. Please take care of yourself and only consume art that you feel you can handle.

With all my love,

Amanda

Chapter 1

Ivy hurriedly unlocked the door and rushed inside. Her blonde hair was soaked. Thankfully, she had decided on a braid this morning. She would have to give it a good redo, but at least she would look as put together as rainy days would allow.

After making sure the door was locked behind her, she made her way to her office. The dim lights that were left on at all times were barely enough to guide her through the dark library today.

Rain had been pouring for days. The sky was such a dark gray it looked like perpetual dusk outside. It would have been a great day to just stay home, curled up with a blanket, with a hot cup of tea, her sweet boy Apollo, and an excellent book.

Unfortunately, half of the small town of Sparrows Ridge thought the same thing. That meant facing the monsoon to check out a cozy read and a few movies. There was no playing hooky today.

Sparrows Ridge, named after the Foxglove Beardtongue flower, sat nestled in the foothills of Alabama. It had a population of about 3,000 people, most of which had never ventured further than the town limits. What had drawn her to this place, she couldn't tell, but this where she ended up and though it lacked a Starbucks, she was happier here than she had been in a long time.

Ivy dropped her purse and lunch on her desk, rubbing her hands together for warmth. While most states enjoyed fluffy snow in January, Northeast Alabama got rain. It was cold enough to freeze on power lines and your car windshield, but rarely enough to give them a good snow day. If there happened to be snow, it was usually gone in a day or two.

Despite that, Ivy loved living here. She was originally from, well, all over the North, where snowy winters were the norm, went to college at the University of Alabama for her Master's in Library

Science, and moved to Foxglove three years ago to become the youngest librarian the town had ever had at the age of twenty-three.

It took the townsfolk a while, especially the older crowd, to give her a chance. The former librarian had been in the position for over twenty years and was a local. Ivy had big shoes to fill. She was an outsider. However, once they realized she had a passion for the library, she was golden. They absolutely loved her.

Ivy could see herself like Ms. Debbie, staying until she retired, watching families expand and children grow.

She shook her head. It was shocking to her that she had been here this long. Ivy was used to moving around. She wasn't accustomed to putting down roots anywhere. It was a product of her upbringing.

After putting her lunch in the staff room refrigerator, and redoing her wet braid, Ivy began to get the library ready for the day.

The library itself was a converted schoolhouse that had been built in the 1800s. There were two levels, with the computers, research area, and activity rooms occupying the upper story. The first floor was books and the children's story time area.

The shelves were hand-built as were the circulation desk and the other wooden displays, which had been handmade by a local carpenter in 1950. It wasn't the biggest library, and it wasn't the newest. In fact, there were a lot of things that needed repaired and replaced, but it was quaint and well-loved.

"God, I thought I was going to drown out there!" Carrie, her assistant, came barreling through the library like a stray bullet.

Carrie Brown was even younger than she was and full of fire. It showed in her presence, in her sharp green eyes and curly red hair. She was a free spirit, born in a time and place that didn't necessarily understand her.

She wore flowery skirts and layers of scarves. The bracelets on her wrists jingled whenever she moved. Carrie's wide-rimmed glasses seemed to take over her entire face, giving her an owl-like look. It didn't matter if Carrie covered her face with her hair and glasses, she was a beautifully striking woman. Ivy often wondered if Carrie could see that herself.

The two of them couldn't be more different. Carrie was spiritual and loved giving people advice based on their astrological sign. Ivy was stoic, logical, and never wore jewelry that would make noise. Her attire was always crisp, a little vintage, but professional.

Still, Carrie was her best friend. They'd hit it off as soon as Ivy walked through the door. Carrie was the one to first believe in her and showed her around town. Ivy was pretty sure that Carrie wouldn't have taken no for an answer on the best friend status even if she had tried. Carrie claimed people and now, Ivy belonged to her extended family.

"You know what that means." Darren came in behind her. "We are going to be swamped today."

Darren was the newest addition to the library. He was an older man, rail thin, and with a no-nonsense attitude. She wasn't sure about his bluntness at first, but he'd grown on her and the patrons.

"Your braid looks nice today," Darren said to her as he shook out of his rain coat.

"Yeah, I'm sure it does," Ivy responded. "Nothing sexier than rain drenched hair."

"Speak for yourself," Carrie groaned, trying to pat dry her curls with a paper towel.

Darren and Ivy couldn't help but laugh. Carrie stuck her tongue out at them and then rushed to the bathroom to see how bad it was.

After finishing up their opening duties, the trio took a moment to enjoy the peace. Ivy enjoyed a nice hot cup of her favorite tea, which she bought at a shop in town, while Darren and Carrie tried a new tea concoction that Carrie had been working on.

"What's in it?" Darren asked.

"Just drink it," Carrie ordered.

"Okay, but it better not give me the poops," he warned.

"That was only one time!"

Ivy laughed until she heard a pull at the door. She groaned when she saw there were already four people waiting outside. They technically had four and a half minutes left, but it was cold and rainy, so her heart softened.

"Ready, guys?" she asked them.

"Let in the horde." Carrie nodded, making her way to the circulation desk with Darren right behind her.

Ivy flipped on the lights on her way to the door. As soon as she turned the key, it seemed like the people outside had multiplied. They came rushing in, shaking off the cold and rain.

"Good morning, Ms. Newton," an elderly patron, Mrs. Isaacs, greeted her. "It sure is ugly out there today. I wonder when it's going to let up."

"Good morning, Mrs. Isaacs," she answered. "I hope sometime soon or we're going to need boats to get around!"

Mrs. Isaacs, who was at the library at least once a week, gave Ivy a hearty giggle. She went to explore the mystery section, as was her norm. Ivy knew she'd find her later in one of the chairs reading her new book. It was mostly because of Mrs. Isaacs' vivacious reading habits that Ivy had to keep the mystery section updated regularly.

Another patron, twelve-year-old Harper, came barreling through. Harper was one of the brightest kids Ivy had ever met. He was an old soul trapped in a preteen body.

"Good morning, Harper," Ivy greeted him.

"Do you wish me a good morning, or mean that it is a good morning whether I want it or not? Or that you feel good this morning? Or that it is a morning to be good on?" he said, speaking like a Shakespearian actor.

"Quoting Tolkien this morning, huh?" She laughed.

"You got it! My brother did not, but I shouldn't be surprised. He's not much of a reader," Harper stated.

"What are we researching this morning?" she asked.

"Rainfall and accumulation history in Sparrows Ridge," he started. "My brother and I have a bet about whether we've ever had a flood and if so, how much and how long it lasted. I say it's never happened here, not in recorded history anyway."

"Interesting," she replied.

Ivy glanced out the rain marked window to see the car that had dropped Harper off. A broad man, one she could just make out, sat in the driver's side. She knew it was Harper's adult brother. She had never met him but knew enough about their situation that she didn't doubt it was him. Harper waved to him, and the car drove off.

Harper ran off to the public computers and started his research for the day.

The rest of the day was chaos. The rain didn't let up; it actually became a storm, which had them without power for over an hour. They had to check out books on paper, and they had no Internet access, but thankfully her staff and the patrons took it in stride.

By the time they were ready to close, Ivy was overly exhausted. Darren and Carrie looked bright-eyed and ready to go. In fact, they had plans for that evening and wanted her to join them.

"You can be old and tired when you're actually old and tired," Darren told her.

"I just want a hot bath and a glass of wine while Frank Sinatra lulls me into relaxation," Ivy countered.

"He can lull me alright, but not to sleep," Darren responded.

They all laughed as Ivy walked away. She politely, but sternly ushered the remaining patrons out of the door, Harper along with them.

"Where's your brother?" she asked.

"He's working," Harper responded.

"You're walking home?" she worried.

"It's completely safe," he reassured her. "I'm twelve and I only live a block away."

"Okay, if you're sure," she said. "I could walk with you."

"No, thank you," he smiled. "See you tomorrow."

"Harper, who won the bet?" she couldn't help but ask.

"Unfortunately, my brother did." He looked let down. "There was a flood here forty-five years ago that wiped out half of downtown. I didn't think I would find the information I needed when the power went out, but the research section has extremely well-kept detail records of our town's history. I am impressed."

"Well, in your defense, you weren't even alive forty-five years ago," she said, then added. "And it just goes to show you, books still have their place in modern society."

"Yeah," he laughed. "Good night, Ms. Newton."

Ivy waved him goodbye and returned to the desk. She was smiling, but stopped as soon as she spotted the look on Darren's face.

"What?" she asked.

"Not that one," he told her.

"What are you talking about?" she wondered.

"You get pet projects with these kids and their families," he pointed out. "Not that one."

"Why not? And I don't have pet projects," she defended herself.

"Yeah, you do, and not that one because he's a Belmonte," he said.

"Okay." Ivy was confused. "Harper is a good kid," Ivy stated, feeling defensive about the boy.

"I'm not saying he isn't a good kid, but he doesn't need saving," Darren told her. "Roman, his brother, is a good guy, he's just…"

"Been through a lot," Carrie chimed in. "Nothing but tragedy follows that family. It's really a horrible story. Roman is a good guy, but it's been hard for him to get out from under the dark blotch of his worthless parents. They were killed in a drug deal gone bad.

Harper saw it all, so that's why his brother has custody of him. It's a hot mess. There's a lot more, too."

Ivy just nodded her head. She had heard plenty of stories about the Belmonte crew but didn't realize it was that bad.

After declining their offer for the hundredth time, Ivy finally headed home.

Most days, she rode her bike to work. She lived two blocks over, so it wasn't far, but it gave her a bit of exercise. Her truck was a mess, but it got her to work on days like today.

She'd had the truck since she was fifteen years old. It had been her birthday gift from her father, one of the last things he'd given her. She tried to keep up the maintenance on it, but the truck, a 1984 Chevy Silverado, was old when it was bought. She was surprised it had lasted this long.

Ivy pulled into her driveway, which was longer than her drive to work. Her house was one of the reasons she just couldn't leave this town. It was way too big for her with four bedrooms, two baths, a study and a den, but it was gorgeous and a steal.

She had done a lot of work to the house when she first bought it. After the repairs were done, the house was absolutely beautiful. There were still some things she wanted to work on, but she was satisfied for now. If she was a different person and had a different story, she could see raising a family here.

She parked the old truck under the carport. She hurried inside just as another deluge started to come down.

As Ivy entered the mudroom, her German shepherd, Apollo, greeted her with a soft, "I missed you," whine and a kiss.

"Hey, bud," she scratched him behind the ear, "I missed you, too. It's a flood out there, so we'll have to get you a bath when you come back in."

She let Apollo out to do his business. He was a muddy mess when he returned. That was one of the reasons she'd had a dog bath put into the garage. After she washed the grime from his coat and dried him off, she led them both inside into the warmth. Apollo found his bed and went straight to sleep.

Ivy drew the hottest bath she could handle and sank gratefully into the water. She tried her best to let the day wash away with the rain, but Darren's words danced around her brain like a ballerina on speed.

"Not that one."

Why not? Wasn't it her job to take the lost under her wing? As the town librarian, she thought so. Heck, as a decent human being, it was her job. It shouldn't matter where he came from or who his family was.

She honestly didn't think Harper was neglected in any way. However, there was something about him that called to her. Maybe it was the haunted look in his eyes even when he smiled. Ivy knew what that was like.

These thoughts were still swirling around her mind later as she lay in bed drifting off. Her last conscious thought was that Harper Belmonte might not be in need of saving, but he might just need someone who listens.

Once a month, Ivy worked the Saturday shift so Darren and Carrie would have a weekend to themselves. Saturdays were busy, but nothing she couldn't handle on her own. She knew the regulars would come in, but it was rare to have anything out of the ordinary happen.

Harper came in about two hours before closing. He didn't look like his normal chipper self, but when Ivy asked him about it, he just shrugged it off and went to the Young Adult section. She thought about asking him what was wrong, but then another patron came in and she didn't have time.

It wasn't until she was closing up that she realized he was gone. She felt like she had let him down. Here she was telling herself she was going to reach out, and she didn't even ask him how his day was. She was off to a brilliant start.

Ivy finished locking up and made her way to her truck. The rain was still falling in steady sheets, bouncing off her umbrella, when she noticed someone sitting on the bench. It wasn't an abnormal event. Patrons would sit out front, using the free Wi-Fi to check emails or Facebook. However, they didn't tend to do it in the rain, and they never looked that small.

She took a few steps toward the figure with the hood pulled up. She recognized the jacket.

"Harper?" she called, walking up to him.

The young boy sat on the bench, shivering. The awning was hardly a shield from the onslaught.

"Harper, what are you doing out here?" she asked him, bracing herself against the cold.

"I just…needed to leave." He stared out at the wet street.

"Come on, Harper," she touched his shoulder, "Let's get you home."

"I'm fine," he responded, pulling his hood down over his eyes. He had been crying.

"I can't leave you out here," she told him, gesturing toward the rain. "Come on."

He sat there for a second longer, but then followed her to the truck. When he got in, he gratefully warmed his hands with the truck's mediocre heater.

"Alright, where do you live?" she questioned as she turned the heat up.

"My brother is going to be so mad at me." He looked worried.

"Maybe not," she offered, patting his shoulder. "Do you want to point me in the right direction?"

He said nothing for a moment.

"The sooner we get you home, the better," she prodded.

"Take a left on Winter Crest," he finally said. "It's the last house on the right."

Ivy nodded her head and drove out of the library parking lot. Harper wasn't lying when he said he lived within walking distance to the library. It took them only two minutes to pull into his driveway.

The house was an older structure, just like hers, but in immaculate condition. This was a street that had been constructed when the town was first built. Harper's house was a classic Victorian home with sharp arches and a wide porch. The only thing modern about it was the workshop that had overtaken the garage.

"Did you know that the Chevrolet pickup's sister truck, the GMC, or 'Jimmy,' was originally produced to be the luxury version of the Chevrolet line, but as Chevys offered more options and appointments through the years, both trucks became almost identical except for the badge identification?"

Ivy looked at him for a moment. He was delaying the inevitable.

"I didn't know that, Harper," she smiled at him gently, "Let's go."

Ivy got out of the truck and walked up the porch steps with Harper. She could have let him go by himself, but she felt it was her adult and professional duty to speak to his brother.

She knocked on the door, and it immediately swept open. A tall, hulking figure filled the doorway. Ivy stepped back slightly in shock as the man's features came into view once the porch light was on.

His black hair was wild, wavy, and narrowly touched his broad shoulders. It looked as though he had been running his hands through it repeatedly. There was a fierceness in his green eyes. It must have been a trademark of the Belmonte family, those expressive eyes with depths she couldn't fathom. He looked from her and then to Harper, his face going from mad to livid. He had a phone to his ear and flicked a Zippo in his other hand over and over.

"Harper!" He grabbed the boy by the shoulders and shook him, dropping the phone. "Don't you ever...Dónde diablos has estado? Huh? What were you thinking?"

"Mr. Belmonte," Ivy interrupted. "Harper was…"

"Who the hell are you? What are you doing with my brother?" He stood up to his full height, which felt well over ten feet. Ivy could tell he was a man that was used to intimidating others. It wasn't something he tried to do; it just came naturally to him. Well, it would not work on her, not after doing the right thing by bringing his brother home. She squared her shoulders and looked him straight in the eye.

"My name is Ivy Newton, Mr. Belmonte," she said sternly. "I'm the local librarian. Your brother was sitting outside when I left tonight. I offered him a ride home since, as you can tell, it is raining and cold. Now that he's back home, I'll leave you two to discuss matters on your own."

She nodded to Harper and turned on her heels and marched back to her truck. By the time she got home, her head was pounding, and she was beyond angry. Of course, Harper's brother had pissed her off, but she was more upset with herself for nearly losing her cool on him.

She thought she was doing the right thing, taking care of Harper. And then his brute of a brother looking at her as if it were her fault.

"Maybe he should keep a better eye on his brother and this wouldn't have happened!" she said aloud, tossing her purse on the counter.

She didn't tell Carrie or Darren what had happened when she got to work on Monday. She didn't want to hear a lecture, and they were too busy telling her about their amazing Saturday, anyway.

Carrie was raving about this new Italian restaurant they'd gone to and the cute server who she exchanged social media contact information with.

"He's a Virgo so I know he'll be kind and sympathetic," she said, checking in books from the drop box. "We're going out Friday night."

"Hopefully not at the restaurant he works at, right?" Ivy teased.

"What? No, of course not." Carrie had taken her seriously. "We're going to watch that new Chris Hemsworth movie and eat at the restaurant in the theatre."

"Well, try not to drool over Hemsworth the entire time," Ivy said, giving her a wink. "You might give the guy a complex." She stood up and stretched. "Hey, listen, I have to get this report done, so I'll be back in Reference if you need me."

"You got it, boss." Carrie saluted her.

Ivy spent most of the day working through her report. Apparently, there were a lot of reference materials that hadn't been returned to the appropriate branch within their system. That meant going through each volume of the report to make sure everything they had actually belonged to them.

She could have gotten Carrie or Darren to do it, but she needed something to distract her mind. Besides, she liked tasks like this. It helped her see parts of the library that needed updating or rearranging.

The only problem with starting this today was she had worn the wrong outfit. She was moving up and down a ladder wearing her snug black skirt, a crisp white shirt, and her mustard yellow sweater over that.

Before she knew it, she was sweating. Ivy took off her short black boots and sweater. She untucked the white shirt and rolled up the sleeves. She put her golden locks into a bun on her head and went back to work.

Around 2:30, Ivy heard, "She's back here somewhere."

She turned from her place on the ladder just in time to see Carrie leading Harper and Roman Belmonte down the aisle.

"Ah, there you are," Carrie said, giving her one of her 'What the?' looks. "Ivy, you have visitors."

"I see." She immediately felt defensive at the sight of the broad-shouldered man.

Ivy began making her way down the ladder when her tights slipped on the bottom rung. She nearly lost her footing, caught herself, and straightened her rumbled shirt as she stood to face them, her face beet red.

"Should we go to my office?" she asked, gesturing toward the front of the library.

"No, this won't take long," Roman answered.

Carrie excused herself as Roman pushed Harper forward.

"Uh, Ms. Newton," he began, his eyes darting from her face to the shelf behind her. "I just wanted to apologize for the situation I put you in the other night. That was irresponsible of me. It won't happen again."

"Thank you, Harper." She smiled down at him. "I'm just glad you're alright. I hope you're feeling better."

"I am, thank you." He gave her a slight smile.

"Harper, go find a book to check out," his brother said. "I need to speak to Ms. Newton."

Harper looked at his brother for a moment and then left for the Young Adult section, if Ivy had to guess.

"Look, Mr. Belmonte, when I brought Harper home—"

"I appreciate what you did for Harper," he interjected.

"I'm sorry." She wasn't sure she'd heard him correctly. She expected that same aggressive attitude, so it threw her off by how easy-going he sounded.

"Harper is a good kid," he told her. "He's a bit different, but hell, who isn't? He didn't mean to put you out the other night. Sometimes he gets in these moods and runs off…and…anyway, I hope he's still allowed to be here. He loves this place."

"What? Of course, he is!" she exclaimed with a small, worried laugh. "He'd have to do a lot more than that to be banned from the library. We enjoy him so much. He's a wonderfully bright child."

"Thank you." Roman looked nervous suddenly. "And I wanted to…uh…apologize for my behavior as well. I was scared out of my mind, so when I saw him…I didn't mean to take it out on you."

"Oh, I understand." She waved him away. "You were worried."

"I wanted to give you this," he handed her a business card. "It has my number on it. I would appreciate a call if Harper has a mind to do anything like this again."

"Of course." Ivy took the card from him.

"And thank you," he told her, catching her off guard once again. "For bringing him home. That was very kind of you."

"You're welcome, of course, anytime," she told him, her mind flooding with a flurry of thoughts.

They stood there for a moment longer, not sure what else to say. Thankfully Harper came down the row just then, saving them from awkwardness.

"I found something." He held up a Manga book.

"Great," Roman said. "Have a good day, Ms. Newton, and thank you again."

The Belmonte boys walked away from her, leaving her confused and a bit jilted at the fact she couldn't hold on to her anger. She wanted to be mad at Roman Belmonte with his untamed hair and knowing eyes. She felt she had the right to be, but now that he had apologized, she felt cheated and almost a little guilty. He was just being a brother. His anger wasn't toward her last night.

Ivy made her way up front just as Harper and Roman were having the book checked out. They both waved good-byes. She waved back and noticed she was smiling.

"What was that about?" Carrie asked after the Belmontes left.

"I thought I said not him, Ivy," Darren chimed in. "What happened? And your bun is all lopsided."

Ivy tried to ignore them and retreated to her office. She fixed her messy hair and put Roman's card in her purse. They followed her, waiting for an explanation.

Ivy sighed and told them about Harper running off to the library.

"And he apologized?" Carrie wondered, looking back at the door as if she would still see Roman. "I've known Roman since high school, and he doesn't apologize to just anyone."

"Well, he was just being an adult." Ivy shrugged.

She remembered the fierceness in his eyes when he had looked at her that night. Only love made people act that way. It was undeniable how much Harper meant to him and Roman wasn't afraid to show it. And the sincerity of his apology also struck her as rather refreshing. He wasn't one to hold back on what he was feeling, it seemed. Ivy shook her head and got back to work. There was a lot to do, and she didn't have time to unravel the mystery of Roman Belmonte.

Chapter 2

Thankfully, the rain had finally let up and Ivy was able to ride her bike to work the next day. There was still a chill in the air, but she was grateful for the exercise. Being outside always gave her energy and helped clear her mind.

She was busy most of the day working on an expense report, but when she left her office, she noticed Harper was back. He was hunched over the computer screen with notebooks scattered around him. A copy of *Hamlet* was opened next to him.

"Are we struggling today?" she asked as she walked up behind him.

"That noticeable?" he remarked, sighing and looking up at her. "I know Shakespeare is supposed to be this amazing writer, but I'm just not feeling it. I mean, this story is bonkers! All this royal treachery, and then there's a ghost? I don't get it."

"Shakespeare isn't for everyone," she agreed. "But he was definitely a talented man who paved the way for many of the brilliant authors we have today. Would you like for me to help you?"

"Not unless you want to proofread my five-page report," he sighed once more.

"I don't mind," she offered. "I have a minor in Literature."

"Really?" He looked excited. "That would be so awesome."

"Sure, just email it to me." She gave him her address. "So, you're in 7th grade, right? And you're already doing research papers on Shakespeare?"

"I'm in AP classes and my English teacher is a Shakespeare fanatic," he explained.

"Ah, gotcha." She smiled.

"I don't know why this class is getting to me." He began formulating an email to her. "I can breeze right through classes, but not this one."

"You can't be too technical when it comes to Literature," she offered.

"What do you mean?" he asked, looking up at her.

"Novels, poetry, plays…they're all art," she explained with a shrug. "They can be subjective. What you felt reading about the death of Hamlet's father might not be what I felt about it. That's why some people love, oh let's say, *The Lord of the Rings* and some don't."

"Yeah." He nodded and then sent her the paper. "But only a crazy person wouldn't love *The Lord of the Rings*!"

"Right you are! Give me a couple of days and I'll get back to you," she told him. "For now, take a break. Sometimes you just need to step away from it."

"Did you know that two of Shakespeare's plays have been translated into Klingon?" Harper smiled at her and then started picking up his things.

"Really?" she laughed. "I did not know that."

"Yep, *Hamlet* and *Much Ado About Nothing* can be enjoyed by Trekkies," he laughed and then found his way to the Young Adult section again.

Soon after, his brother came to pick him up. It surprised Ivy that he actually came into the library. Darren and Carrie watched as Roman gave Ivy a small wave and then left.

"I think he's sweet on you," Carrie commented, watching Roman leave. "If he weren't so broken, I'd so go for it. He's hot as hell."

"Broken?" She gawked. "Really, Carrie?"

"There is so much you don't know," she said.

"I don't want to know." She plugged her ears and walked into her office.

Not that she was interested in Roman in any way, but she didn't think it was fair to judge him and Harper based on their past. What if Carrie knew about her past? Would they still be friends?

Ivy left the library that evening and headed to the local grocery store. She made a quick stop by her house to get her truck. She only needed a few things, but it was more than the little bike basket could handle and the temperature had dropped a few degrees from that morning.

The bike had never failed her at the Farmer's Market on Saturdays, but it wasn't a grocery getter and she needed dog food. If she came back without dog food again, Apollo would disown her; she knew it.

Ivy grabbed a cart and headed down the first aisle to her right. She was not one to peruse the grocery store. She actually hated shopping in any form unless it was for books or things for her house. She always had a list, and she would check things off in record time to get back home.

The thing about having plans was that they never worked out like they were supposed to. She ended up running into her pastor, her hairdresser (who told her about her aunt's friend's cousin's dog that got hit by a car), and the school librarian, Mr. Archer.

"We have to get you in the school again!" Mr. Archer said to her as they talked in the baking aisle. "The children just enjoy when you read to them."

"I do as well." She smiled, her face straining.

It's not that she didn't like Mr. Archer. He was a nice man, but Ivy could tell he sort of liked her. He had, in so many words, asked her out. Granted, it was to the church luncheon, but Ivy had still had to find a way to let him down gently. He wasn't her type at all.

"Just let me know and we'll get it set up, Mr. Archer." She smiled again.

"Now, Ivy, I've told you before, just call me Blake." He smiled back at her. "You know, I was wondering…"

Oh no, here it comes, she thought.

Blake, with his overly animated facial expressions and too strong cologne, was going to ask her out again. It wasn't going to be to the church luncheon either. She had to find a way out of this conversation—and fast. She could fake a call, or maybe faint. Or she could just woman up and tell him she wasn't interested.

"Ms. Newton!" she heard a familiar voice from down the aisle.

She turned to see her guardian angel. Harper came rushing toward her, his big hulking brother trailing behind him. The young boy nearly gave her a hug, but then thought better of it. Harper had never been very affectionate. She didn't think it was because he didn't want to be. He just had trouble knowing *how* to be.

"Well, hello there, Harper." Ivy kept her hands to herself, tempted to pat the boy's shoulder.

If Harper didn't want to touch her, she wasn't going to touch him. Harper would figure out if he wanted a hug or a handshake, and she'd be glad to extend him either one.

"Hi, Ms. Newton!" he said again. "Hi, Mr. Archer. Look here, Roman, two librarians in one place."

"I hope it doesn't create a riff in the space-time continuum." He smirked, his green eyes bright with amusement.

Was he joking? Did this big, stoic guy know how to joke? Ivy gave him a look, one eyebrow raised and a grin.

"How are you doing, Roman?" Blake asked, reaching to shake his hand and Roman finally took it after a long awkward moment. "It's been a while. It's funny, Roman and I graduated together, live in the same small town, and yet hardly see each other."

Blake laughed as if he had just told the funniest joke. Ivy gave him a smile out of sympathy, but Roman just sort of glared. Ivy was pretty sure that was his resting face. There was no telling what was going on behind those green eyes.

"Well, I really better be going." Ivy grabbed her cart handles, ready to go.

"Oh, but Ivy," Blake began.

Really, Blake? In front of these guys?

"Mike and Emma's wedding is next weekend and…"

"Oh, yeah, heard about that," she told him as she continually backed up. "Too bad I can't go. See you all later."

She took off down the aisle, leaving them in her dust. She was certain she had seen Roman trying his best to restrain a smile. Ivy grabbed the rest of her items from the list and made an unscheduled stop down the wine section. She grabbed a bottle of Riesling and headed for the register. Thanking her lucky stars she didn't see anyone at check out, she hurried to her truck.

Ivy was putting her bags into the truck when Roman came up behind her. "I'll get that for you."

He grabbed the dog food before she could say anything and put it in the bed of the truck. She was tempted to ask him if he was going to follow her home and get it out, too, but she refrained. Ivy had been lifting dog food for as long as she'd had Apollo and had been doing just fine. She decided to keep that to herself as well because she was sure he was just trying to be nice.

"Thank you," she said.

"Ms. Newton, have you looked at my paper?" Harper asked her, leaning out of the car window next to her.

Ivy had been so preoccupied getting into her car that she hadn't realized who was next to her.

"I have," she told him. "I'll be finished with it this evening and send it back to you."

"Great," he told her. "Your hair looks pretty like that. Bye!"

The young boy climbed back into the car and rolled up the window.

"Bye, Harper," she laughed.

"I think that's our cue to leave…before someone else attempts to asks you out," Roman said, hiding a grin, and nodding to her. "Ms. Newton."

Ivy stood there, unsure of what to say. So, he had noticed that Blake was trying to ask her out. She felt her face flush, but she wasn't sure as to why.

Ivy spent the next few days trying to avoid Blake at all costs. He would call her at work, send her emails, or just show up. She had hoped that her avoiding the topic of going to the wedding and completely brushing him off would be a clue, but she was wrong. Carrie and Darren were no help at all. They thought it was endearing.

"I mean, he's not a bad-looking guy," Carrie told her as she scrolled through Blake's Facebook page. "Those are in short supply around here."

"Yeah, well, good looking or not, I just don't have any connection with him," Ivy told her. "I need to let him down easy, but I don't know how."

"Just say you're not interested," Darren suggested. "Simple and to the point."

"I know, you're right." Ivy was busy dusting their circulation desk. "I just...don't want to cause tension between us. We do a lot of programs together for the kids."

"Blake seems like a reasonable guy." Darren grabbed the cleaning cloth. "And we have a cleaning lady for that. Go be a librarian."

Ivy sighed and headed back to her office with Carrie's voice following her, "I think you should give him a chance!"

Ivy had zero plans of dating anyone. When she'd moved here, it wasn't to settle down and have a few kids. Her career was her marriage, and the patrons were her children. She wanted to see this place grow.

In her previous life, there was no growth. Her father died and her mother...well, there was a reason they didn't speak. She was tired of living in darkness, and she was done with settling for anything or anyone. She wanted a life that was bright and full of the possibility of something more. That's why she had chosen this little town. Sure, everything had its bad blood, but the people here, most of them, were good, caring people.

And if she wanted to start a relationship with anyone, it wouldn't be with someone she had just friendly feelings for. She might want love someday, and it would be passionate. He would make her blush and smile even when she didn't want to. He would stir her heart, make her want to feel things, and she wouldn't be able to stop thinking about him in bed. That wasn't Blake. It wasn't anyone.

Ivy called in a dinner order that night before she left. Rita's was the local diner with some amazingly greasy food like burgers, fries, and everything heart attack inducing. It also had the best veggie club sandwich Ivy had ever tasted. She even added a few chicken fingers for Apollo. He would never forgive her if she showed up with Rita's and didn't bring him anything.

The first time Ivy had gone to Rita's she felt like she had been transported to a 1950s classic diner. It had all the appropriate furnishings: the tall bar with swivel barstools, the booths with high back benches and glittery plastic cushions that squeaked when you sat in them, a juke box, and a checkered floor. Ivy loved it.

Rita's was a walk down the street, so she wheeled her bike over and leaned it against the side of the building. She had no thoughts about locking it up. In this town, her bike was safe. Besides, if someone was that desperate to take her old school-looking bike, with its second-hand tires, they could have it.

The bell jingled over Ivy's head as she entered the diner. The smell of freshly grilled burgers and fried bacon greeted her, making her stomach grumble. It was strange that she enjoyed the smell of cooked meat, but not the taste. Ivy had been a vegetarian since she was ten and then added fish around 14. She approached the counter, ready to pay for her meal.

"Ivy, it's going to take us just a few minutes to get your chicken fingers up," Taylor, the cashier, told her. "Sorry, we had a big order just before you called."

"Oh, that's alright." She smiled. "I'm not in a hurry."

"Do you want a soda while you wait?" Taylor asked. Her plump rosy cheeks looked a little extra rosy today.

"I'll take a sweet tea," Ivy told her.

"Coming right up." Taylor ran her debit card for the order.

She handed Ivy back the card and went to get her tea. Rita's didn't skimp on the food or drinks in her establishment. Taylor handed her giant Styrofoam cup filled with the best sweet tea around. There really was nothing like this tea anywhere. She was addicted and unashamed.

As Ivy was about to take a seat in the waiting area which was just three chairs between the door and jukebox, she heard someone call her name.

"Ms. Newton!" She turned to see Harper waving at her.

She smiled and waved back, taking a big gulp of her drink. Her heart flipped at the sight of Roman as he turned to look back at her. He looked different. Maybe he had trimmed that unruly hair and full beard.

"Ms. Newton!" he called again. "You must come over."

By this time the entire diner was looking at her. In order to avoid more stares, she walked over to the booth that Harper was sharing with his brother.

"Well, hello, gentlemen." Ivy smiled.

"Ms. Newton," Roman greeted her with a nod. "I feel like we keep running into each other. Are you stalking us?"

"What?" She was confused for a moment. "Oh, very funny."

For a moment Ivy stared at him. He actually had a small smile for her, which seemed to reach his eyes. Her stomach felt a bit odd for a moment, but then she looked at Harper as he started talking.

"We're out celebrating," he told her.

"Oh, really? What's the occasion?" She couldn't help but grin at his enthusiasm.

"I made an A on that paper." He beamed. "Your help was no doubt the reason."

"He was so excited about it when he came home," Roman looked at her, "I had to get him out of the house or I was afraid he might explode, taking me and the house with him."

"Well, I am so happy for you," Ivy told him. "But I only gave you a few pointers. You did all the work."

"Are you eating here?" Harper asked.

"Oh, no, I'm just waiting on my order." Ivy pointed to the front.

"Do you want to sit down while you wait?" Roman offered.

"I don't want to impose on your celebration." Ivy felt her face flush a little. What was going on with her?

"It's not a problem, really," Roman insisted.

"Yeah, Ms. Newton, please sit." Harper moved over so she could sit down.

"Well, alright, thank you." She sat down with them.

For the next few minutes, Harper told her all about his paper and how she had made it so much better. Ivy listened and smiled. She would occasionally look up to see Roman staring back at her. Each time they made eye contact, she felt her stomach drop. Maybe she was hormonal after watching *Pride and Prejudice* last night. Any woman was going to feel all swoony after watching Mr. Darcy woo Elizabeth.

Taylor finally brought her order to her and apologized for the wait. It just so happened that the boys' order arrived just after. Ivy couldn't help but notice how Taylor kept her eyes on Roman. Was she jealous? Did they have a thing going on? Ivy pushed those thoughts from her head. It was none of her business.

"You have to stay and eat with us now," Harper told her. "It would just be weird if you left."

"I agree," Roman chimed in. "Super weird."

"If you're sure I'm not interrupting family time," she said.

"Not at all." Roman smiled.

Ivy opened her veggie sandwich and was glad Taylor had remembered to put the chicken fingers in a separate container. She placed the chicken fingers inside her bag. She looked up and noticed the boys were staring at her.

"They're for my dog," she explained and felt her face redden. "I don't eat meat, not since I was a little girl. Well, I eat fish. Apollo, my dog, he loves Rita's chicken fingers."

"I can't say that I blame him," Roman laughed.

It was a hearty laugh that made Ivy's skin tingle. She laughed, too, glad they didn't think she had a thing for sticking chicken fingers in her purse.

Roman and Harper didn't grill her about her eating habits, which was a tremendous shock. Anytime she revealed that tidbit of information about herself, she was peppered with questions. It didn't seem to matter if she told people it was her preference, they tried to tell her it must be from a terrible experience from her childhood. Or that she "didn't know what she was missing."

They did, however, ask her all about Apollo. Harper had been asking for a dog for the last year. Roman would agree only if Harper would start remembering to pick up after himself. Apparently, he was the absent-minded professor. Harper wanted to know everything about Apollo.

"He was my mother's dog," Ivy told him, the words spilling out of her mouth. "He wasn't very well taken care of, so when I left for college, I took him with me."

She normally just told people that Apollo was a rescue. It wasn't a lie. He was malnourished and abused. Her mother had no business trying to raise anything. She couldn't even take care of herself, much less a defenseless animal.

"I'm sure he appreciates that." Harper smiled.

"I like to think he loves me just a little bit," Ivy told him, taking a bite of her sandwich.

"I don't doubt it," Roman agreed.

The trio ate and chatted, laughed, and joked. Ivy was thoroughly surprised by how much she was getting along with Roman. They had a lot in common, she found out, as far as movie tastes and music. They both enjoyed a good classic rock song, but Harper was fine sticking with his Broadway musicals and Disney soundtracks.

Before she would have liked, it was time for her to leave. She would have to warm up Apollo's chicken, so she hoped he wasn't too mad at her. Stacey, their server, came over and dropped off the check for Roman. Ivy couldn't help but notice how her eyes lingered on his face and how much it looked like Stacey wanted to choke her. Dear God, did he bang every employee at Rita's?

Stacey didn't have anything to worry about. Ivy was no threat to her pursuit of Roman Belmonte. She knew Stacey only by eating at the diner. She had always been kind to her, but Ivy knew the kind of girl Stacey was; she had seen plenty. She'd smile to your face and talk about you behind your back. Her long blonde hair and full lips, large breasts and a small waist were definitely head-turning, but Stacey was one of those girls that would just as well slap you as she would hug you.

The group left the diner and Ivy grabbed her bike from the wall. She was telling them goodbye when Roman offered her a ride.

"Oh, I'm fine," she insisted. "I do this all the time. I only live just down the road."

"Yeah, well, it's a bit late," he told her, his eyes staring intensely at her. "People around here can hardly drive in broad daylight."

"I don't think my bike can fit in your car," she said, remembering his muscle car.

"I drove my work truck tonight." He gestured to the white pickup parked up the sidewalk. "Please, I don't mind."

"Well, okay, thank you," Ivy relented. It didn't seem like he was going to take no for an answer.

Roman rolled her bike to the truck and placed it in the bed. It was a single cab truck, with the words Parker's Home Construction. Ivy got in after Harper and sat by the window.

"Parker's?" she asked Roman. "They worked some on my house."

"I know," he told her, pulling away from the curb. "I was on the crew. I'm one of the foremen now."

"Really?" Ivy was shocked, surprised she hadn't realized it before.

"Yeah, I was just one of the grunt guys, working on the backsplash," he confessed with a laugh. "I'm sure you don't remember me."

"I... think—I think I do," Ivy recalled. She could see Roman and another man working in the kitchen. "Your buddy kept trying to get my number."

"You do remember," he laughed. "That would be Max. He's a character."

"Definitely," Ivy said. "Well, character or not, you guys did an outstanding job on my kitchen. I've done a lot in the house myself, small things, but you guys were amazing. I can see why you were promoted."

"Thank you," Roman said to her, cutting a grin her way.

Harper yawned loudly between them. The young boy was extremely tired. His sleepy green eyes matched Roman's perfectly. You would almost think he was Roman's son, not his brother.

They pulled into Ivy's driveway in no time. She was thankful she'd left a light on inside so she wouldn't be walking into complete darkness. Apollo was barking from the backyard because he didn't recognize the sound of Roman's truck.

"Can I meet him?" Harper asked.

"It's late, buddy," Roman told him. "Maybe another time."

"Can I, Ms. Newton?" he wondered. "When it's daytime."

"Of course you can," Ivy said. "We'll set something up. And now that we've had dinner with one another, I think it's time you and your brother call me Ivy."

"I'd like that." Harper smiled. "Goodnight, Ivy."

Harper hugged her, and she slid out of the truck. Roman got her bike out and handed it over to her.

"Goodnight," he told her with a small smile. "Ivy."

A tingle went up her spine. Ivy quickly nodded and headed up the porch steps. She entered the house and let Apollo in through the back door. He huffed at her for being late but soon forgave her once he realized she had chicken fingers for him. Ivy took a shower and crawled into bed, Apollo beside her. As she fell asleep, she remembered that small tingle of her skin caused by Roman's smile.

Chapter 3

It was another cold and rainy day when Ivy awoke the next morning. Winter was digging in and not letting go. January was halfway through, but it appeared it was trying to either freeze them or drown them. She let Apollo out for a bit, but he rushed back in as soon as his business was done. On days like this, she let Apollo stay in the house while she was at work. He was a good dog and never made a mess.

The library that Ivy managed was part of a vast system. It was shown support from a large organization, but it still saw little income from the group. Most of its funds came from the town of Sparrows Ridge, which meant her boss was none other than the mayor. Mayor Cliff Turner had been the mayor for over twenty years and the high school science teacher for fifteen years before that. He was a well-liked man with a lot of pull in the small town. Ivy understood why. He was a good person who cared about his fellow residents of Foxglove.

When Ivy had interviewed with him, he hadn't gone easy on her. He wanted to make sure she knew what she was getting herself into with such a small branch. Mayor Turner had wanted to know everything about Ivy. He'd asked her why she was here, why she wanted to be a librarian, and what she had planned for the branch. She was a bit intimidated by his questions, but apparently answered them all to his liking, because she had an offer in her inbox the next day.

"You won't be paid much, but we will make sure it's enough to pay your bills," he had told her. "It's not glamorous, but we adore this library."

"I'm not looking for glamour, sir," Ivy said with honesty.

"What are you looking for?" he asked.

"A home," she said and then felt as if she had shared too much. "A home library. A place where people want to come because they love it."

Cliff was a tall, slender man with stock white hair and deep brown eyes. He had such a deep voice that surprised most people at first. If Ivy was being honest, he reminded her a lot of her dad with his love history, how he decorated his office in sports memorabilia of his favorite college football team, and the kind way he spoke to her.

It was no surprise to her when she came into the library that Mayor Turner was there. He was wearing his jeans and a work shirt. Ivy had asked for someone to look at their A/C unit. Mayor Turner enjoyed getting his hands dirty and was a bit of a handyman.

"Good morning, Ivy," Mayor Turner greeted her.

"Good morning, Mayor Turner," she walked up to him, her bag on her shoulder. "What's the verdict?"

"It looks like the system just needs a flush," he said as he used a screwdriver on the unit vent. "I'll get the workers over here this evening to get it done. We'll do it after you close so the noise won't interrupt any programming or patrons today."

"I appreciate it, Mayor, thank you," Ivy said. "Are you staying for the meeting?"

"Of course," he said, wiping his hands on his work cloth. "I would never miss your presentation."

Yes, her presentation. She was nervous this morning. Ivy had been working on this proposal for the last seven months. Today was the day to present it, and it was go big or go home. One thing about small towns, they normally didn't like change, and what she was proposing was a pretty significant one.

Ivy excused herself and locked herself away in her office. She had less than thirty minutes to do any last touch ups before the monthly Friends of the Library meeting. The Friends were patrons of the town. They were mostly an older group who had retired and had time to volunteer and fundraise for the small library. Some of them even made large donations each year toward the function of the branch.

She hit it off with most of them. They were good people who wanted nothing but what was best for the branch. However, there were a few who thought just because they gave money, that their opinion weighed more than others—especially hers. Still, she was hoping they were open to her suggestions.

"Hey." Sawyer opened her office door. "Are you ready?"

She had reached out to Sawyer Miller a few months ago. He worked at the main branch in the library system and was a Sparrows Ridge local. He was a whiz with the financial side, with projections and estimates. He had been a CPA in another life. The two of them had hit it off and become fast friends when she had first started working for the library. Working together on this project had been seamless.

"It's time already?" She gulped, standing and smoothing out the lines in her grey skirt. She had opted for a black turtleneck, low heel shoes, black tights, and a fitted at the waist skirt. Now she thought maybe the turtleneck was a bit much because she was sweating.

"Deep breath." Sawyer came in and grabbed her shoulders, "You look great. You're going to have a great presentation and blow everyone's mind."

"Right," she breathed. "Let's go."

Ivy greeted everyone as she walked to the front of the table. There were a lot of "Good morning" and "How are you?" in return. The Friends was a group of twelve: eight women and four men. They ranged from ages 47-63. The youngest, Felicia Coleman, was the President and someone that Ivy considered a friend. She'd tried to keep the Friends at arm's length at first, separating her professional and personal life, but Felicia just wouldn't let her.

Felicia owned the local flower shop with her husband, Patrick, who was also on the board. She'd had dinner at their house, been to their children's basketball games, and even to a pool party.

"Good morning, Ivy," Deacon Ross, the mayor's nephew, greeted her.

"Deacon." She nodded, trying to keep the disdain from her voice.

Deacon Ross had that country boy charm with big city attire. His sandy brown hair was cut short and sleek, and Ivy admitted to herself that he was dashing in his $2,000 suit. He cut his bright blue eyes at her; the way he had the first time they'd met three years ago. It had taken him some time, but he'd finally convinced her to go out with him. She didn't want to mix business and pleasure, but he was smooth and won her over.

At least for the first six months of their "relationship." Ivy was never one to open her heart to a man very easily, and it was even harder to open her bed. Still, they were like hormone fueled teenagers for a while. They couldn't get enough of each other. That was until she caught him face deep in his secretary's thighs, in his office of all places.

His excuse? He didn't know they were "exclusive." Ivy ended things and prayed that the mayor wouldn't find a reason to fire her. Thankfully, Mayor Turner knew exactly how his nephew was. Her job was secure, and Deacon was kicked to the curb.

Unfortunately, Deacon was also their district's representative. That meant that Ivy had to see him at meetings like this and community gatherings.

She pushed those thoughts away and focused on the task at hand.

"Thank you to everyone for coming out on such a dreary day," she started. "I know this isn't our normal meeting day or time, and as you're all well aware, because word travels fast in a small town," —laughs, that was a good start— "you know I have something exciting to share with you and, hopefully, get your support."

Ivy looked at Sawyer, and he began handing each member a sleek black folder. Ivy had spent the last few weeks making sure every detail about that folder was perfect and correct. Her heart beat wildly in her chest as the council members opened them.

"I wanted to bring to your attention today about how much our library has grown," she began, trying not to pull at her turtleneck.

"On this first page you will see membership from five years ago and what number we are at today. Not only has our membership grown, but so has our attendance in the programs we offer. For example, our Summer Reading program was fifty kids five years ago; today we have two hundred. We have so many that we must use City Hall's meeting room instead of our facility. That can sometimes run into issues, especially if the city officials plan to use that space at the same time. We had to cram into the children's area, which you know can hardly hold one hundred, on a good day."

Ivy stopped for a moment to let everyone take in the information she had given them. They looked at her knowingly, not saying anything, and so she proceeded.

"That is just one of many examples," she told them. "I have detailed other capacity issues in the report you have in front of you. I know you can all read, so I won't go through each example unless you just want me to. I say all of that to say this, after spending the last seven months, along with the help of Sawyer Miller, I have come up with a proposal for expanding the library."

The members looked at her with wide-eyed expressions. The library had been the same for over one hundred years. Nothing had changed in their lives and with the library begin such a staple in the town, this was shocking to them.

"Ms. Newton, our library has a certain...charm," a member, Mrs. Webb, chimed in. "How would your proposal ensure that our history would be preserved?"

"You are completely right, Mrs. Webb." Ivy had been expecting this question. "If you look on page fifteen, you will see the proposed changes, none of which would remove any historical items in this library. This is an expansion, not an overhaul. As you can see on the diagram, the building would be expanded on the right side, and in the back. It would move the parking over and actually increase parking space."

She spent the next twenty minutes going through each detail of the expansion. It was going well until Mrs. Webb spoke up again.

"This all sounds, um, wonderful, but I'm curious as to the price tag of this...expansion," she said.

"Right," Ivy was not bothered by her condescending tone. "On the last page, you will see a detailed breakdown of the cost and a list of donors who are already willing to contribute."

"You've already talked to outside sources, before talking to us?" Mrs. Webb questioned her.

"Well, yes," Ivy continued. "The community is forever in the debt of the Friends, but with all due respect, I had to talk to the city council about the logistics, costs, and so on because, well, they own the building."

The old woman's face went as red as her bottle-dyed hair. She flipped to the back and looked at the numbers.

"Two million?" another member, Roger Waters, asked. "And that's an estimate?"

"Yes, sir, that's correct." She felt like she was losing ground here. "But as you can see from the list of donors..."

"Ms. Newton," Mrs. Webb chimed in again, her smile smug on her face, "We love the work you do here, but you're...not a native Sparrows Ridgeian. I don't know what your plans are for the future here, but once you're gone, we will be the ones left with your...changes. Two million is a big number."

"I am not a native, you're correct about that," Ivy told her, this time her hands moved to her neck before she forced them by her sides. "However, your mayor and the county hired me to do my best job here. That includes pointing out when...changes...as you put them, need to be made. I can promise you that through our donors, and fundraisers, we will reach the number you see on that page. And, if you must know, I have no plans of leaving Sparrows Ridge, and if I did, like my daddy taught me, 'Ivy, whatever you do in life, wherever you work, you make sure you leave it better than you found it.' That's what I intend to do with my position here."

Deacon cocked an eyebrow at her as if to say, "Well done, Newton." Sawyer was concealing a grin. No one said anything for a moment, and finally Felicia spoke up.

"Ivy, you have done amazing work here," she began. "I, for one, am in full agreement with this proposal. I'm not saying it won't be without its challenges, but I know we can reach that goal if we all work together. After all, the purpose, in fact, the mission statement of this group contains the line, '…in pursuit of sustainability, and growth, of the Sparrows Ridge Library.' We have been long overdue a proper event and meeting room if I do say so myself. While you do not need our permission, I am glad you have sought our approval, Ivy. I make a motion to fully support this endeavor in a capacity that this board is capable of. We will have our treasurer look at our records and see what we can do to contribute, and then meet again to discuss fundraisers. Do I have a second?"

"I second," Roger spoke up.

"All those in favor?" Felicia asked; almost everyone raised their hand. "Those opposed?"

Mrs. Webb and her best friend Mrs. Foster raised their hands. They were clearly outnumbered but didn't care.

"Motion passed." Felicia gave them a certain look. She was such a diplomat but didn't stand for it when someone didn't have the library's best interest at heart. "Please note that Mrs. Webb and Mrs. Foster oppose this endeavor."

The secretary nodded her head and wrote the notation in the minutes. The two older ladies were red faced and as soon as Felicia adjourned the meeting, they didn't stick around to talk to anyone.

"Don't worry about those old bats." Felicia came up to her with a warm smile. "Some people don't know how to handle change. This is definitely exciting, Ivy. I can't wait to see what comes of it."

Felicia gave her a hug and followed the other members out of the library. Deacon was lingering, talking to his uncle. Ivy sighed. She had to find a way to get him out of the library.

"I'll get those, Sawyer, don't worry about it." She began moving chairs, helping Sawyer.

"I don't mind," he smiled, still working. "You did such an amazing job, Ivy!"

"Thank you," she said and stopped to look at him. "I couldn't have done all of this without you."

"I just crunched some numbers," he laughed.

"Well, it was the best number crunching ever," she joined in with a laugh of her own.

Just then Deacon excused himself from talking to Roger and made his way toward them. He grabbed a few chairs and helped.

Dear, Lord! Ivy thought. If Deacon was helping, then he really wanted to talk.

They worked the next few minutes in silence, and then finally they were done.

"Thanks, guys," she tried to sound nonchalant. "I really need to…"

"Do you have a moment?" Deacon asked before she could finish. "I need to discuss a few matters with you about your proposal."

"Um," she began, looking at her watch. "Yeah, about five minutes."

"I'll, uh, see you later, Ivy." Sawyer looked from Deacon to her.

He knew about their history, and he didn't like Deacon at all.

"Yeah, okay, Sawyer. Thanks again." She gave him a warm smile.

She watched him leave with Roger. Ivy led Deacon to her office, making sure to leave the door wide open after ushering him in.

"What's up?" she asked him.

"First, that was a great presentation." He sat in the chair across from her desk.

"Thank you," she said, even though she didn't need his approval or praise.

"You're welcome." He gave her one of his most charming smiles, his eyes lingering on her lips.

"You had a question?" she prodded, not in the mood for his games.

"Right," he cleared his throat. "It's not really a question, more like a suggestion. Have you talked to Youling about donating? I saw they were not on your list of contributors. I didn't know if they came across your mind when you were reaching out to people."

Youling was one of the biggest companies in the next town over. It developed and researched all sorts of technology. Ivy wanted to roll her eyes so hard. Of course she had reached out to them. However, getting in contact with the right person at a company that big, and untouchable, was next to impossible.

"They were at the top of my list, actually," she said as professionally as she could. "I probably talked to about fifteen different people before I finally realized they either didn't want to help me or didn't know who I should talk to. So, I moved on."

"Really?" Deacon looked surprised. "Well, I actually play golf with the VP of Operations at Youling. I could either talk to him for you or give him your contact information."

Ivy's ears perked up. As much as she wanted to gag at his "I play golf with the VP" remark, she would be insane not to take him up on his offer. Still, Deacon rarely did anything out of the goodness of his heart.

"What's in it for you?" she couldn't help but ask, crossing her arms.

"What do you mean?" He actually had the gall to look offended.

"You do amazing things for this town, Deacon, but you always make sure everyone knows it was you who did them." She narrowed her eyes, staring him down. "So, what do you want in return?"

"Ivy." He stood up; she stood up as well. "I'm just offering to help. I swear, that's it. I mean, can't I do a favor for an old friend?"

"Friend?" she scoffed.

"There was a time we were more than that," he reminded her, walking around the desk. "I know I messed that up. I'm just trying to find a way to get back into your good graces."

"Don't do this for me," she pointed at him, "Don't do this for yourself. You do it for the town and don't take credit for it."

"Okay, fine," he threw his hands up, smiling, "I won't mention it to anyone but you and Butch, the VP. I promise."

He crossed his heart like he was a fifth-grade girl, making a promise not to tell anyone her best friend's secrets.

"You can give Butch my contact info, but if you want to take him the proposal and speak to him on our behalf, then I trust you." She handed him a proposal folder. "Don't make me regret it."

"I promise," he said and stood there looking at her for a moment. It was as if he wanted to say something but thought better of it.

It was a good thing because she could hear Carrie and Darren making their way through the library. Deacon smiled and then excused himself from her office.

"Well, hello, stranger," Darren greeted him.

"Darren. Carrie. Good to see you both." He nodded at them as he made his way toward the exit.

When he left, Carrie and Darren spilled into her office. They knew all about their passionate love affair when Ivy had first arrived. Thankfully, only a few people did. It was a small town and news like that spread like wildfire. Deacon had actually been gentlemen enough not to go around talking about how he had bedded the town librarian.

"It was just a professional meeting, guys," she told them before they could ask.

"Good," Carrie said. "He might be easy on the eyes and loaded to the gills, but he's a two-timing man-whore."

"Tell us how you really feel, darlin'," Darren said. "I, for one, think he's matured, but a little too late. Now that Sawyer fellow…"

"Oh, Sawyer is a cutie pie if I ever did see one," Carrie agreed.

"Alright, you two." Ivy busied herself with making a cup of hot tea.

"What?" they said in unison and looked equally innocent.

"I don't need a matchmaker," she told them. "And Sawyer? No. We're just friends."

"Someone needs to tell him that." Darren grabbed a soda from her mini fridge.

"The boy has it bad, Ivy," Carrie chimed in. "You'd better let him down easy."

"You guys are crazy," Ivy laughed. "Sawyer is not interested in me. I'm pretty sure he has a girlfriend."

"Well, a girlfriend isn't a wife," Darren remarked. "But are you sure you don't want to give him a shot? Not all men are pigs like Deacon."

Just then the library doors opened. They hadn't locked the doors after the meeting. It looked like their day was going to start early. Ivy didn't complain about the interruption either. She was done talking about Sawyer, and Deacon, for that matter.

If Ivy could see herself, maybe one day, with a husband and a few kids, it wouldn't be Deacon or Sawyer lying next to her at night. It was highly unlikely it would be anyone from this town, and definitely not anytime soon.

Every time she thought about settling down and having children, her heart would stitch up. Ivy's upbringing had been challenging, to say the least. Her father had passed away when she was twelve. He was her entire world.

For twelve years, he was all she had known. After he died, the state gave her absentee mother full parental rights. Her mother, Linda, was a drug addict and only cared about when she got her next hit.

For years, Ivy suffered at the hands of her neglect. If it wasn't her handprint across Ivy's cheek, it was that of Linda's latest boyfriend.

Ivy swore if she ever had children, she would do anything for them. They would never be scared in their own home.

When Ivy turned eighteen, she found out her father had left her an account with enough money to pay for her first year of college. That, along with a few scholarships, helped pay for Ivy's education. He had also left her a truck with one of his best friends. She was glad her mother never knew about any of it, or she would have cleaned her out and sold the truck.

As soon as she left for college, she never looked back. Her mother had tried to contact her, but Ivy didn't return her calls. She wasn't into social media, so after moving to Sparrows Ridge, Linda had no way of finding her—she hoped.

It was for the best. As an adult, with a lot of emotional baggage, she was afraid of what she might say or do if she saw that woman again.

Chapter 4

Ivy and Sawyer were pouring over the proposal for the extension late into the evening that Monday night. A very prominent socialite wanted to meet with them the next day, and they wanted to make sure they had missed nothing.

Mrs. Margaret McNair, the daughter of Alabama Senator John Henderson and married to an Alabama District Judge, was born and raised in Sparrows Ridge. When she wasn't a philanthropist in third-world countries, she enjoyed contributing to her hometown.

Ivy had reached out to her several months ago and was surprised to get a call from her office requesting a meeting, and that meeting was to take place the following day, at the library.

To say Ivy was a ball of nerves was putting it mildly. Margaret McNair was her second dream contributor, Youling being her first.

Deacon hadn't spoken to her about it since he offered to talk to their VP of Operations. It had only been a week, so Ivy tried not to think too much of it. She trusted him, but only because Deacon loved rubbing elbows with the big dogs and the big dogs liked donating. It was a good tax write off, and it made the rich feel good about themselves.

Ivy rubbed the back of her neck. She had been hunched over this proposal for far too long. If it wasn't sufficient by now, then it probably never would be. Still, she was a masochist and a self-doubter.

Sawyer must have sensed her unease because he looked up at her from his place across the desk.

"Are you hurting?" he asked.

"What?" She was confused for a moment. "Oh, I must have just slept funny or something. I took an Aleve, but that was," she looked at her watch, "about fourteen hours ago."

"We should call it a night." He yawned, stretching his arms, and then scratched the stubble on his chin. "You have an important meeting and I have toddler story time first thing in the morning. We both need sleep and lots of it."

"Yeah, I suppose you're right," she agreed. "But, do you think…"

"Ivy," he reached over and grabbed her hand, "This proposal is rock solid. You've done amazing work here. It's as good as it's going to be. The only thing you need to do is just be yourself. The numbers and calculations are important, yes, but what really matters is that our donors see how much you love this library. They're going to get infected with your passion and before you know it, we'll have all the money we need."

Ivy looked at him and then at his hand on hers, which he didn't seem like he was going to move anytime soon. She wondered if Carrie and Darren were right about his feelings for her. It made her nervous, but then he pulled his hand away. Sawyer clearly didn't like her. He really was just a good guy.

"Well, thanks for comparing my passion for the library to an infection," she laughed and felt suddenly lighter. "But you're right, we've done all we can do for tonight. I need to go. I'm sure Apollo is pissed at me for leaving him outside so long."

Ivy began gathering her things. Sawyer watched her for a moment, smiled, and then started picking up himself.

"Do you need a ride?" he asked as they began walking out of the building.

"No, I drove today." She gestured toward the pickup truck as they rounded the corner to the parking lot.

"Ah, ol' Trusty." Sawyer laughed.

"Hey! Don't make fun of my truck," she punched him. "She has never let me down."

"Ok, ok!" he laughed, holding up his hands in surrender. "But when that bucket of bolts finally gives out, please let me take you truck shopping."

"Whatever," she rolled her eyes. "That truck is probably going to outlive us both."

They stopped in front of her trusty steed as Sawyer looked at it as if he just needed to put out of its misery.

"Stop judging her," she laughed. "She's been through a lot."

"I see." He smiled as Ivy dug out her keys. "I'm parked just over there. Call me after your meeting tomorrow. I want to know everything. You've got this, Ivy; don't doubt yourself."

She nodded her head, wished him goodnight, and then climbed into the truck. Ivy had to make a quick pit stop by the store. She had nearly run out of lunch food and deodorant. She didn't want to worry about pit stink during her meeting tomorrow. Why she didn't remember to pick some up the other day was anyone's guess. Too much on the brain was her excuse.

She had to drive nearly twenty-five minutes to the only store open at this hour. Yawning as she pulled into the parking lot, Ivy hurried into the store. The temperature seemed to have dropped another few degrees.

She sped through the store, got what she needed, along with a few things she didn't, and ran out. As Ivy was heading back home, eating the candy bar she really didn't need, she decided to take a back road. It was quicker and after chugging the soda she'd bought, she really needed to pee. As she took her last bite, the truck gave a lurch.

"What the?" She nearly choked.

It sputtered a few times and died. Ivy tried not to panic as she guided the truck to the side of the road.

"Shoot, shoot, shoot!" she said as she came to a stop. "Sawyer jinxed us! Or maybe it was me. Come on, girl!"

The truck was indeed ancient and probably needed to be retired, but it had always been pretty reliable until now. She turned the key again and again, but nothing happened.

She popped the hood and got out to look. Using her phone's flashlight, she scanned the motor. She was no mechanic, so she seriously doubted she could figure out what was going on by staring at the engine in the freezing cold.

After getting back in the truck, Ivy grabbed her phone and called Sawyer. Hopefully, he wasn't asleep already. It went straight to voicemail. Just then it started to rain.

"No! Seriously!" she moaned. "Okay, truck, you can do this. Come on."

Ivy sent up a little prayer and turned the key again. Nothing.

"Ugh!" She hit the steering wheel.

She tried calling Sawyer again. And again, no answer.

She called Carrie and then Darren, multiple times, and neither one of them answered. There was no way on earth she would call Deacon. She'd walk home first. It was possible she would have to do that.

Ivy figured she could wait until the rain stopped and walk down the road to see if anyone was home at the next house. There weren't many down this stretch of road. But who knew when the rain would let up to do that?

What if the resident of that house was a serial killer? She didn't want to go out like that.

It seemed her only option for the moment was to try calling a towing service, which she didn't want to do because her insurance wouldn't cover it.

She began digging in her purse for chewing gum as she debated if she could afford to shell out a hundred bucks when her hand ran across a card—Roman's. He had given it to her the other night while they were talking.

She stared at it for a moment. Would it be weird to call him for help? She shivered as the cold seeped through her coat. Desperate times called for desperate measures.

She punched the number into her phone and hit send. As soon as it started ringing, she hung up. It was nearly midnight. Surely, he was asleep and if he weren't, he would probably be royally ticked off that someone was calling him that late. Besides, he barely knew her. Being driven home from a block away and getting rescued from the side of the road were two different things.

Her phone buzzed in her hand. It was him! Roman. He was calling her back. He didn't know it had been her calling; he didn't have her number. Who called back strange numbers that hung up after one ring?

She debated not answering, but she felt if he ever found out it was her that had called, it would embarrass her. She was already embarrassed enough as it was for reaching out to him.

"Hello?" she answered nervously.

"Ivy?" His voice was rough, as if he had been asleep. She felt terrible. "Is everything okay?"

"I am so sorry, Roman," she started. "I know it's late, and I've called everyone I know. If you can't help, I understand…"

"Ivy, what's going on?" he asked.

"My truck broke down." She felt defeated.

"Tell me where you are; I'll come get you." He sounded wide awake now.

"Are you sure?" she asked. "It's so late. And what about Harper?"

"Ivy," he said sternly.

"I'm on Older Gap Road," she relented.

"Okay, I'm on my way," he told her. "Hang tight."

"Okay, thanks." She hung up the phone.

Twenty-five minutes later, Ivy saw lights coming down the road. A large towing truck and another truck pulled in behind her. Roman and another man exited the vehicles and walked toward her.

She stepped out into the rain, thankful she had her umbrella, meeting them at the hood.

"You brought a towing truck?" It surprised her as he ducked under her umbrella with her.

His bulky frame barely fit. He was so close; she could smell faint traces of his cologne and see the green of his eyes reflecting the light of the truck behind him.

"I figured it would be a lot easier to just tow it than try to figure out what's wrong with it in the pouring rain," he explained. "Come on, let's get out of here. You can ride back with me."

Ivy grabbed her bags and purse and they hurried to his pickup and got in. Ivy often wondered if umbrellas were worth it most of the time. By the time she closed it and pulled it into the car, she was just as wet as if she hadn't had one at all. Rainwater was all over her and the leather seats of Roman's truck.

"Here, I figured you might need this." He handed her a towel. It was small, but perfect to dry herself off and wipe down the seats.

"Thank you," she said as they pulled onto the road. "For everything. I shouldn't have called and bothered you at such an hour. I really am sorry."

"Will you stop apologizing, Ivy," he laughed. "That's what friends are for."

"We're friends now?" She couldn't help but smile, looking over at him.

Dear God, was she flirting with him?

"Sure," he grinned. "I mean, if you want to be."

Was he flirting with her?

"I'd like that," she told him.

Yeah, she was flirting. She had to stop, like, right now.

"You didn't have to wake Harper, did you?" she wondered.

"He's actually at my cousin's house for the night," he explained. "If I have to work late, like tonight, he stays with her. She has two boys, so Harper enjoys hanging out over there. They're twin boys and three-years-old. Harper loves them."

"That's great," she smiled. "I'm glad he didn't have to be disturbed in the middle of the night. I would have felt really awful. I feel bad enough waking you up."

"Meh, I was just kind of lying there," he smiled at her. "I was thankful for the distraction."

Ivy had to stop her mind from picturing Roman just lying in his bed, wild hair and shirtless.

"So, you had to work late?" Ivy asked.

"Yeah, my crew is on a deadline to finish the new shopping center on First Street." He stifled a yawn.

"Oh, yeah, I saw that," Ivy commented. "It's looking great. I guess we're both burning the midnight oil."

"What are you working on?" he questioned.

Ivy told him about her goal of expanding the library and explained about her meeting with the senator's daughter.

"Wow, that's pretty amazing, Ivy." He sounded genuinely impressed. "I'm really glad our town has someone like you as the librarian. You care, and that's not an easy quality to find in many people these days."

"Thanks, Roman, I appreciate that."

Before long, Roman pulled into her driveway. The tow truck pulled in behind them. She showed the driver where to put her truck and then dug into her purse for her checkbook. As much as she didn't want to, she'd have to pull money from her savings to cover the payment, and hopefully she'd have enough to pay for whatever needed fixing on her truck.

Roman left shortly afterwards, seemingly confident that Ivy was in excellent hands.

"How much do I owe you?" she asked Larry, the tow truck driver.

"It's been covered." He waved a hand. "I just need you to sign this, stating the vehicle was delivered to your place of residence."

"Covered?" She was shocked. "How? By wh—Roman paid you? No wonder he hightailed it out of here."

"I just need your signature." He smiled at her, obviously not willing to divulge any information.

Ivy sighed and signed the contract. She would have a talk with Roman later. For now, she needed to let Apollo out, take a shower, and get something that resembled sleep. The meeting with Mrs. McNair would be here soon enough.

Ivy woke up a little bit later than she had planned. Not that late, but she must have hit her snooze without realizing it.

Her head was hazy, and she swore her eyes looked like she had two saddle bags strapped to them, but she tried her best to cover it with makeup. She had never been good at applying the stuff. Her mother never took time to teach her and what she did know, she learned from a college friend. Still, it was enough to get by most days.

Rain was coming down in sheets. She had fourteen missed calls from Carrie. Ivy needed a ride this morning, so she called her back. She thought about exacting a bit of revenge and letting her worry, because she probably already was, but she would feel too guilty. Carrie would have never ignored her calls on purpose.

Soon, Carrie's canary yellow VW bug pulled into the carport of her driveway. Ivy hurried out the door and got into the warm interior of the old car.

"So what the hell happened?" Carrie asked her, looking concerned.

"Let's get on the road, and I'll tell you everything," Ivy laughed.

And Ivy did just that. When Ivy told her that she was forced to call Roman, Carrie's jaw dropped to her chest. They were at the library by this time and halted their conversation until they'd made it safely indoors from the rain.

"He paid for the tow truck?" she asked again.

"Yeah, I guess he did." Ivy was still mad about that.

"And judging by your expression, you don't like that?" she questioned.

"I don't need anyone's charity." She felt defensive, busying herself with turning on her computer.

"Maybe he was just being nice?" Carrie offered.

"Uh huh," she murmured.

Ivy helped Carrie start up for the day, checking in the items in the book drop and then putting them back on the shelves.

She told herself there was no sense in trying to stress over the proposal anymore. Like Sawyer said, it was as good as it was going to be.

Her phone rang in her sweater pocket. Fishing it out, she saw it was Sawyer. She must have conjured him up with her thoughts.

"Hey," she answered.

"Ivy, I am so sorry I didn't answer your calls," he said. "Are you alright?"

"Yeah, yeah, I'm good," she said and explained what had happened the night before.

"So how did you get home?" he wondered.

"Roman came to get me. He called a tow truck and everything," she replied.

"Roman? Roman Belmonte?" He sounded thoroughly surprised.

"Yep," she answered as she put the last returned book on the shelf.

Carrie was unlocking the door as patrons began to enter. Her heart dropped when she saw Margaret McNair enter behind some of her regulars.

Sawyer was in the middle of saying something, but Ivy cut him off.

"I have to go, Sawyer. She's here." Ivy's mouth felt dry.

"What? Who?" He was confused.

"Margaret McNair." And with that, she hung up the phone.

Ivy straightened her skirt and then made her way to Margaret. She was chatting with Carrie at the circulation desk when she arrived.

"Here is our fearless leader." Carrie beamed.

"Mrs. McNair, welcome." She shook Margaret's hand, a hand that was adorned with a stunning ruby ring and perfectly manicured nails. "I'm Ivy Newton."

Margaret wore a silky green stylish shirt and a pair of dark denim jeans. A pair of ankle books that looked impeccably clean, despite the muddy conditions outside, covered her small feet.

"Ivy, please, call me Margaret," she told her. "And I apologize for getting here so early. I drove in last night and had dinner with some old high school classmates. I woke up at five, just couldn't sleep, and I thought, why not get this day going early? I hope you don't mind. If you are too busy, I can come back."

There was no way Ivy was letting her leave. She hadn't been expecting her until later, but she couldn't be more prepared than she was now.

"No, now is perfect," Ivy assured her. "Would you like a tour?"

"That would be great." Margaret smiled.

Ivy showed her around the library, which didn't take very long. When they were done, they sat in a pair of armchairs by the children's area. She made sure to go into great detail about the functioning of the library, the services they provided, and the love the library received from the community.

"Ivy, I grew up in this town," Margaret started. "And I spent a lot of time in this library. Not much has changed other than...a certain vibe. I'm thinking that vibe is you."

Ivy's heart dropped. She loved her job. She loved this library and the people of this town.

"Margaret, I can assure you that I have the library's best interests at heart," Ivy began.

"Oh, no, no, no," Margaret reached over and patted her hand, "Perhaps I should have worded that differently. You've brought life back into this place. It was always a sanctuary for me, and welcoming, but this is different. It's new and open and appeals to many walks of life. I could tell by the people who walked through the door."

Ivy was a bit surprised. In fact, Ivy was surprised by Margaret herself. She was expecting a posh, stuck-up southern belle. Instead, Margaret was a breath of fresh air and downright likeable.

Margaret shadowed Ivy for the rest of the day. She observed as Ivy ran her homeschool book club for local families, taught a class to the elderly on how to use their computers, and helped a group of recently laid-off factory workers with writing a resume.

"Our foundation is run by a group of generous individuals," Margaret told her. "We spend way too much time, in my opinion, deliberating which programs are worthy of our donations."

Ivy nodded her head, understanding the red tape, and politics, that go along with nonprofit organizations.

"I've talked to many of them already," she continued. "And I'm hoping our decision to donate to your expansion doesn't take nearly as long as usual."

Ivy was walking Margaret toward the exit. It was nearly 5:00. Surprisingly, Margaret had wanted to stay the entire day. She and Ivy had even had lunch together at Rita's Diner.

"And, if I have anything to say about it, this donation will be a sure thing." Margaret smiled and gave Ivy a wink. "But you didn't hear that from me."

"I won't breathe a word," Ivy whispered conspiratorially.

When Margaret left, Ivy did a tiny victory dance back to the circulation desk. Carrie was grinning, watching Ivy try to contain her joy.

"I'm assuming things went well?" Carrie laughed.

"Yes, very!" Ivy exclaimed. "I don't want to speak too soon, but this expansion almost feels like it's going to happen."

"It is!" Carrie agreed. "We have to speak positive vibes into our lives. God, the universe, the great Creator will hear it."

Ivy laughed. Usually, Carrie's hippy vibes were something she'd brush away. Right now, she was feeling pretty positive. What would it hurt to give in a little to the possibility?

The door of the library opened then and in walked Roman and Harper. Ivy's smile didn't falter, but she could feel a bit of irritation crawl up her back.

She knew Roman was being a good guy, but she didn't like the fact that he had paid for the wrecker. He hadn't even asked. She didn't like being in debt to anyone.

"Hey, Miss Ivy," Harper greeted her.

"Harper, how are you?" she asked with a smile and then looked at his brother.

"I'm fine," he said. "We came to check on your truck."

"Is that so?" she asked Roman.

"Yeah, I have a friend who is a mechanic," Roman started. "I'm sure he'd give you a good deal on whatever's wrong with the truck. But, um, I thought, if you wanted me to, I could look at it. I'm known to be pretty handy."

Ivy was surprised to see him look sort of nervous. He shuffled his feet and his big, tall frame moved from side to side.

"Roman—" Ivy started, but Carrie cut her off.

"Hey, maybe you could give Ivy a ride home then?" Carrie suggested, and Ivy whipped her head around to look at her.

Traitor.

"That way you could take a look at her truck."

"Yeah, I could do that," Roman offered. "If you'd like?"

Ivy had been fully ready to tell Roman off. Now, as she looked at him and then at Harper, the wind was taken out of her sails. She wouldn't rip him a new one, at least not here. It wouldn't be very professional.

"Sure, that sounds great," she finally relented. "Thank you. I just need to gather my things."

"No problem," Roman smiled widely. "We'll just wait here."

"Carrie, a word?" Ivy walked away and into her office.

"Yes, boss?" Carrie asked innocently.

"What was that?" Ivy wondered, her hands on her hips. "Weren't you and Darren warning me against getting too close to the Belmontes?"

"I was," Carrie walked a little further into her office and whispered, "but I was reading my cards last night…"

"Oh, Carrie," Ivy sighed, rubbing her hand down her face, forgetting she was wearing mascara today. It was probably smudged now.

"And you were on my mind," Carrie continued. "And the cards never lie. You are supposed to trust a stranger this week."

"He's not a stranger, Carrie." Ivy began packing her belongings into her purse. "And where were your cards when I needed a ride last night?"

"Hey, I only know what they tell me." Carrie threw her hands up. "And it's not nice to make fun, Ivy."

"You're right," she said, grabbing her umbrella. "I'm sorry, but I'm still mad at you."

"You'll thank me later." Carrie smiled.

"Whatever." Ivy rolled her eyes and walked out of her office.

Roman and Harper were waiting on her right where they said they would. She greeted them with a smile and let them lead her out to...Roman's muscle car?

Ivy was completely expecting his work truck. She had forgotten about seeing him in this thing.

Her knowledge of cars in general was very limited. What she did know was this car was very sleek, very loud, and could go very fast.

"I hope you don't mind." Roman opened her door, noticing her expression as she took in the automobile.

"What? Oh, no, it's fine." She smiled and got into the passenger seat.

Harper got into the back, which was just one long seat. She was sure that four full-grown adults could fit back there, and quite comfortably.

"Nice car," Ivy commented as they drove down the road.

"Thank you," he replied. "Even though you don't mean that. I can tell you don't like it."

"What? I mean it," she laughed. "I mean, I wouldn't drive a...what is this exactly?"

"It's a 1964 Pontiac GTO," Roman told her. "I rebuilt the engine myself. It took a while because some of the parts were... You don't care about this do you?"

"I wouldn't say that," she told him. "I just know nothing about cars, so you might as well be speaking another language."

"Don't worry, Ivy," Harper said, leaning forward. "It's not just you. Roman brags about this car to everyone who will listen. This car is practically his girlfriend."

"Funny, Harp." Roman looked at him through the review mirror.

"It's true!" Harper defended himself. "If he's not at work, he's in the garage doing something to this car."

"Well, we all have a passion, right?" Ivy tried helping.

"Yeah, see," Roman agreed. "We've all got something we like to do, a hobby."

"I play crossword puzzles," Harper confessed. "Yeah, it's nerdy, but I like them. What about you, Miss Ivy?"

Ivy sat there for a minute and thought about what she liked to do other than work.

"Um, read, I guess," she offered. "Surprisingly, I don't get a lot of time to do that."

Soon they pulled into her driveway. Roman's car rumbled up the drive and parked next to her dead-as-a-doornail truck.

"Can I meet Apollo?" Harper asked excitedly.

"Of course," Ivy said as she got out. "How about you and I let him run out back while your brother checks out my truck? Let's go get my keys."

"Okay!" He hurriedly raced up her porch steps, beating her to the door.

Roman smiled as he followed behind them. Ivy unlocked her door and gave entrance to her home to the Belmonte brothers. She couldn't help but feel as though that one action changed something.

Apollo was eagerly waiting for them to enter. He wagged his tail and whined as they came into the foyer.

"Sit, Apollo," Ivy commanded, and the dog obeyed. "This is Harper and Roman. You can say hi now."

Apollo shot over to them, sniffing their feet and allowing them to pat his head. He ran between them, unsure of who he wanted affection from at the moment.

"Come on, let's get you outside," she called, and Apollo followed her to the sliding glass doors in the back.

The large dog took off as soon as the doors were open. Harper wasn't far behind him. Ivy left the two to play while she fetched Roman her keys.

She handed them to him and said, "Let's go see what the damage is, Belmonte."

Roman got out his toolbox and started looking over Ivy's truck. She leaned against the wall of the carport, watching him work. She could also see Harper and Apollo in the backyard. It was a clear vantage point to all the things she wanted to monitor.

Ivy watched Roman as he maneuvered around the hood's interior like he had done this a million times. His face was a mask of concentration, but relaxed. He was clearly in his comfort zone. He reached over to mess with something, and Ivy couldn't help but notice how the sleeves of his long gray thermal shirt stretched across his muscled arm.

Roman was not a small man. He had to be at least 6'2" with a broad frame that didn't seem the least bit out of shape. His dark, shoulder length hair was straight, but full of volume. It seemed to feather around his chiseled features in the most seductive way. Ivy called it model hair. Bad boy, run your fingers through it and get lost hair.

"What's the verdict, Doc?" she asked in order to distract herself from her current train of thought.

He closed the lid and wiped his hands on a well-worn cloth. "Well, looks like your alternator died."

"How much is that going to run me?" Ivy dreaded the answer.

"If you get a mechanic to replace it, around $300," he told her, walking up the carport to stand in front of her. "My buddy might do it for $250. If you buy it yourself, it'll probably be around $100, and I can put it in for you."

Ivy was taken aback by this generosity. She remembered the tow truck and narrowed her eyes at him. What was his agenda? It was rare in her experience that men wanted to "just help."

"I could pay you," Ivy said.

"It's no sweat," he said, looking down at her. "I could change an alternator in my sleep."

"Well, I need to at least pay you for the tow truck." She turned and walked toward the side door. "I didn't mean for you to cover that. I can pay for myself," she finished as she entered the warm house.

She knew she'd said that with a bit more venom in her voice than she had intended.

"Ivy, I didn't mean to offend you." Roman stood at the entryway to her living room. "A buddy owed me a favor, and you've been so good to Harper...I just wanted to help. No money exchanged hands if that's what you're worried about."

Ivy stopped rummaging in her purse for her checkbook and looked up at him.

"Oh, well, thank you." She felt a little embarrassed for being so defensive. "I don't need repayment for anything that concerns your brother though, Roman. That kid is—he's amazing. I'm glad to be a part of his life."

"Well, thank you." He smiled. "So... Are you okay with me replacing your alternator? I can get the part ordered through my friend's shop. You can pay for it when it comes in."

"Yes, that will be great." Ivy stood looking at him as if she'd never truly seen him before.

"What?" he asked after a moment.

"Huh? What? Nothing. Do you want to stay for dinner?" she blurted out.

"Sure, yeah," he cleared his throat, smiling. "Sounds good."

"You can wash up in the bathroom over there." She pointed to the guest bath behind her.

Roman nodded, walking past her. The faint smell of his cologne and leather drifted along with him.

Ivy excused herself to get out of her work attire before she handed out any more spontaneous invitations. When she returned, her long blonde hair was in a simple braid that reached the middle of her back. She had exchanged her tights for black yoga pants and her cardigan for a comfy sweater.

Since Ivy didn't eat meat, and only had fish on hand, she didn't know what else to feed them. She had perfected a recipe for a nice baked fish a long time ago. It would have to do, she hoped.

"Do you guys like white fish?" She poked her head into the dining room where Roman and Harper had set up a game of Uno, just to be sure.

"Yeah, we're not picky," Roman responded. "No allergies on our part."

Ivy nodded her head and went back to work. She spiced up the fish with olive oil and a few fresh herbs from her indoor herb garden. Ivy liked having them readily available on the windowsill above her kitchen sink. She had always been able to make anything grow, even if a plant was on its last leg. In the spring and summer, her yard was full of flowers and plants, colors bursting and smells that dazzled. It made her feel like maybe she was a woodland witch in a past life.

As she began chopping up vegetables to steam, she heard laughter from the next room. She leaned a bit over the kitchen island and could just see them as they giggled over the game.

"Another Plus Four?" Roman exclaimed. "You're killin' me, smalls!"

Ivy planted herself back on her heels, smiling. Their laughter was warm, infectious. It made her feel something, and the closest word she could think of was *safe*.

When the food was eaten, their bellies full, Roman helped Ivy clean up even though she told him he didn't have to. Upon his insistence, he rinsed as she put the dirty dishes into the dishwasher. Harper sat in the living room with Apollo, throwing the dog one of his many chew toys.

"I like hiking," Ivy suddenly said. "And gardening. But I really like hiking."

"What?" Roman looked over at her as he was rinsing a pot.

"You guys were talking about hobbies earlier," she reminded him, taking the pot from his hands. "I do like reading, of course, but I really enjoy hiking. I used to go all the time, with my dad. I haven't been in ages. I loved it."

"Hiking is fun," he agreed. "I can't remember the last time I've gone and done anything outdoorsy."

"I should go more often," she said, but talking more to herself. "I stopped when my dad passed."

"I'm sorry. I didn't know," Roman said softly.

"I was twelve," she remembered. "Heart attack. He was always so healthy. Crazy," Ivy sighed as she put a washing tablet in the dishwasher and closed it, "I guess you just never know." She looked up at him.

"Yeah, I guess not." His eyes searched her face.

They stood there for just a moment, looking at each other. Ivy was surprised by how easy it was to talk to him. She hadn't spoken about her dad to anyone in a long time.

"Would you like a drink? I have tea or coffee?" she offered.

"I would, but I have to get Harper home." Roman looked reluctant to go. Or maybe she just hoped he did. Yeah, he needed to go.

"Right, of course," she said.

"Another time, maybe?" he said. Or was he asking?

"Yeah, that would be great," she replied, but she wasn't sure if she was actually agreeing to anything. "Good luck getting Harper and Apollo to part."

Roman laughed as he followed her into the living room. Luckily, there were no sad goodbyes because Harper had fallen asleep on the couch, Apollo nestled next to him. Ivy was pretty sure she had never seen anything so cute in her entire life. Roman nudged Harper awake, but practically had to carry the kid to the car. Waving goodbye, she was fully aware of the stupid grin on her face.

Chapter 5

Roman did exactly as he'd promised and replaced the alternator in Ivy's truck. After that, she hadn't seen him or Harper. It had been a week, and she felt odd about it.

The night he came over to change the alternator, she'd offered him a cup of coffee for his hard work. He had come alone; Harper was at a friend's house. Roman had politely refused and left. She wondered if she had done something to offend him but couldn't think of anything. He had seemed so welcoming the other night at dinner, and that night, he was completely shut down.

What bothered her the most was the fact that it bothered her at all.

Ivy was busy in her kitchen when she heard a knock on the door. Her heart quickened. She wondered if the mere thought of Roman had conjured him up at her doorstep. She hurried to the door and yanked it open without even checking to see who was on the other side.

"Deacon?" She was disappointed and knew it.

"Hey, can I come in?" he asked. "I have some news."

"And you couldn't have called?" She crossed her arms, not moving from the threshold.

"I could have." He grinned. Perfectly straight white teeth filled his mouth. "Come on, Ivy, it's freezing out here."

"You have five minutes," she told him and let him inside.

He stepped past her and stood by her fireplace where he warmed his hands. Apollo looked up at him from his bed, ruffed, and then laid back down. Even Apollo didn't have time for him and that made her love her fur baby even more. Ivy stood in the middle of the room, arms still crossed, and stared at him.

"Four and a half minutes," she warned.

"Jeez, okay," he laughed. "I talked with Butch about your proposal. I'm sorry it's taken so long, but there isn't too much golfing going on this time of year. I had to catch him at a luncheon the governor put on."

"It's fine." Ivy wanted to roll her eyes. She always hated it when he talked about rubbing elbows with the local high rollers.

"Anyway," he continued to warm his hands, "He took the proposal and finally got back with me. He's all in. He wants to make a personal donation, but he also wants to host a fundraiser, a gala. He's already in planning mode, wants it around Valentine's Day, and wants to meet you as well. He said he would love your input."

"Are you serious?" Ivy couldn't contain her excitement and moved closer to him by the fireplace. "You'd better not be pulling my leg, Deacon, or so help me God."

"I'm not! I swear," he laughed as he threw up his arms in mock defense. "This is huge, Ivy."

"Holy cow." She felt as if she were dreaming. "Thank you, Deacon."

"All I did was give him your proposal," he told her. "You did all the work. You're...you're pretty amazing, Ivy."

He looked at her with longing in his eyes. Deacon took a hand and brushed her hair from her face. She wished he could be a different guy. There were moments in their "relationship" when Deacon acted like an actual human being. That's when Ivy imagined some sort of future together. However, those moments were few. And, despite what he said, no one could change that much.

"Deacon," she backed away from his touch, "Don't."

She could see the pain in his eyes. It hurt her for him, but it didn't take away what he had done.

"You got it, Ivy." He smiled before dropping his hands to his side and putting them into his pockets. "Butch, or probably his assistant, should call you soon to set up a meeting. He'll probably want me there. I hope that's okay."

"Of course," she told him.

"Well, I guess my time is up." He looked intensely at her.

"Yeah, I guess so." She gestured toward the door.

The next day Sawyer was sitting across from her desk. She had immediately texted him after Deacon left to meet her at the library the following day.

"Seriously?" Sawyer clapped his hands.

"According to Deacon, yes," she said, smiling. Ivy had also told him about her meeting with Margaret.

"So, we have not just one, but two major contributors?" Sawyer was amazed.

"Potentially, but it seems that way." She didn't like getting her hopes up, or his, but she had to share this information with him. He had helped her so much.

"Wow," he said and sat back in his chair. "Good job, Ivy. I mean, seriously."

"I couldn't have done it without your help," she told him. She meant it.

"I just crunched numbers," he shrugged. "You did everything else. This was your idea."

"Well, still," Ivy said. "Your help, your support, it has meant everything to me. So, thank you."

"We should celebrate." He stood. "Some friends and I are going to see that new Stephen King adaptation. You should come with us."

"I don't want to intrude." Ivy hated being a third wheel.

"You wouldn't be," he assured her. "It's just a bunch of overworked and underpaid school staff and librarians getting together for a well-deserved night out."

"Well, how could I say no to that?"

"You should invite Carrie and Darren," he suggested. "It'll be fun."

It had been a while since Ivy had been out with anyone. She knew most of the teachers Sawyer said were coming, and she worked with the other people, so she didn't feel any pressure of having to meet new people.

She didn't mind meeting new people if it was work related. She knew how to be professional. It was her personal life that was the issue. For some reason, she was sure it was childhood trauma, she had trouble in more intimate situations. That's probably why Deacon could not tell how she truly felt about him. That didn't excuse his behavior, but she understood his confusion.

Ivy threw on her favorite black skinny jeans and her Doc Martens. Her gray sweater, which she bought back in college, had Darth Vader in the center. It looked like a super pricey sweater that some sorority sister would wear, but it was the nerdiest thing she owned. She loved it.

She put on more makeup than usual and drew her cat-eye style liner a shade darker. It really brought out the electric blue of her eyes. It was a Saturday night, and she rarely got to dress up, so she paired it with a red lipstick she'd bought a few weeks ago but hadn't had the nerve to wear.

Sawyer came to pick her up at 7:00. They carpooled in case one of them wanted a couple of drinks at dinner.

"Wow, you look great," Sawyer said when Ivy opened the door.

"You're too nice." She smiled.

"Are Carrie and Darren coming?" he asked.

"They had plans but said thanks for the invite," she answered as they got into his car.

"Ah, that's too bad," he truly did look let down. "Looks like you're stuck with me, Newton."

She wouldn't deny that Sawyer was a very attractive man. His sandy blond hair curled at the ends, giving him a boyish charm. He had a killer smile and accompanied with his southern gentleman mannerisms, any girl would swoon.

Any girl except Ivy. While Sawyer was clearly a catch and would make the perfect husband someday, she could only see him as a friend.

They pulled into the restaurant a short while later and found a few people were already there. Quinn Russell, the football coach, and his girlfriend Amy Lawrence, the math teacher, were sitting at a table set for several people. They greeted each other and then sat down with them.

"Where are Kate and Zach?" Sawyer asked.

"You're not going to believe it, but they both came down with the flu," Amy said, sipping on what looked like a fruity margarita.

"Oh, no," Sawyer said. "It got them, too? It's running rampant in the schools."

"Kids don't know how to wash their damn hands," Quinn said in his gruff voice, perfect for a football coach. "Hell, neither do adults. This is why a tiny, microscopic bug is going to wipe us out. Are you worried about a third world war? Don't be. You know, we're overdue for a plague by a few hundred years. I mean, a global one. We've only avoided it because of modern medicine. Well, those little bugs are smart. Pretty soon we're going to get a mutated one that we don't have a vaccine for and BAM—pandemic."

"Oh, no," Amy took another sip of her beverage and whispered to Ivy. "When he gets started on plagues he never shuts up. He's sickly obsessed with them. No pun intended. I think he wants a pandemic just so he can prove that he's right."

Ivy laughed and looked around at her companions. Four of them, including her. Two men, two women.

Oh no, oh no!

It was like a double date! They were even sitting at the table like couples on double dates do. She was panicking. Sawyer could not get the wrong idea about tonight. Did he have the wrong idea? She had agreed to come because it was a group of people. Was she panicking for nothing? Carrie and Darren were getting in her head.

Wait, Kate and Zach were a couple. Had he asked her out, and she didn't realize it? Great! No, no way. Sawyer had never once made any moves or indicated he liked her. She was being paranoid. They were just friends. But did everyone else know that?

Maybe she shouldn't let what people thought bother her, but like it or not, she was a public figure in her small town. People liked gossip in small towns just as much as anywhere else. She was lucky in keeping her involvement with Deacon a secret. She probably wouldn't be that lucky again if she started seeing someone, so she didn't want anyone to think she was with Sawyer and then suddenly someone else. Not that she was looking, but goodness, this was stressing her out.

Ivy ordered an apple martini when the server arrived. As soon as they brought it out to her, she downed it and ordered another one. She was going to need a bit of help to make it through the night.

As they continued chatting, she thought about faking ill so she could just go home. Everyone else had the flu. Why not her? Right at that moment, a dark head of hair caught her eye.

"Roman?" she called louder than she meant to.

The table's occupants stopped talking and looked up. Roman was walking by with two other people, the hostess apparently leading them to a table. One of his companions was his buddy Max. He was a tall lanky fellow with a close-shaved head and dark skin. His rich dark eyes looked from her to Roman with interest.

The other person, a woman, was striking. Her brown hair hung in beautiful full strands around a very gorgeous face. She seemed practically poured into her jeans, and her silky, low-cut top accentuated her full figure. Her sharp green eyes stared at Ivy with copious amounts of curiosity.

"Ivy." He smiled at her after his initial shock of being yelled at in the middle of a crowded restaurant subsided.

"Hey," she said after a moment.

"Hey," he said back with a sly smile.

He knew she had embarrassed herself. She hated how he could read her so well. And, if she were being honest, she kind of liked it, too.

"Um, what are you guys up to?" she asked. "I mean, besides eating. You're obviously at a restaurant, so you must be doing that, right? Eating."

She was babbling like an incoherent toddler. She averted her eyes and took a big gulp of her martini. Crawling under the table to die of humiliation was what she really wanted to do.

"Ha, yeah," he laughed as everyone continued to stare at them. "We're going to watch the new horror movie afterwards."

"Oh, cool, us too," Sawyer chimed in, and Ivy felt like hugging him. "Eva? Is that you? I haven't seen you since high school. The last I heard, you were living in New York, right? Working on Broadway."

"I still am. I'm just visiting for a few months, in between shows." Her sing-song voice was magical.

"Sawyer, everyone, you guys remember Max Cunningham, right?" Roman offered.

Everyone nodded their heads and waved at Max. It was like a Sparrows Ridge High School reunion, and Ivy was the new kid.

"Why don't you guys sit with us?" Quinn offered gesturing at the table. "There's plenty of room. Some of our party couldn't make it, and we could all catch up."

"Sure, yeah, thanks," Roman took a seat beside Ivy.

She could feel the warmth of his body as he sat down, his shoulder brushing hers. He smelled like leather and aftershave. It was oddly comforting.

"Sorry, do you have enough room?" He looked over at her.

"Oh, yeah, I'm good," she said, even though she was cramped between him and Sawyer.

"You're the librarian, right?" Eva asked from her seat across the table.

"Yes," Ivy responded, nervous under her intense gaze.

"I thought so," she said, a slight grin on her gorgeous face. "When I think of librarians, you're not what I picture at all."

"What do you picture?" Ivy wondered with a laugh.

"Oh, you know, the stereotype: enormous glasses on a little old lady with a tight bun on the top of her head." She giggled, and it was damn sexy.

"Sorry to disappoint," Ivy giggled. "I'm sure I'll get there one day."

"Well, for now, you're the hottest librarian I've ever seen," Eva told her, making Ivy blush.

"You just became my new best friend." Ivy smiled, raising her glass and taking another drink.

"Hey, if you're done flirting with Ivy, the server is ready to take your order," Roman said to Eva, his voice light.

"Well, when a woman looks like that she deserves to be flirted with." Eva winked at her, and Ivy laughed, glad this didn't feel like a date anymore.

That was until Sawyer tried to pay for her meal. She could see Roman grinning from the corner of her eyes. She wanted to smack him, hard. She knew Sawyer was only trying to be nice, but it was giving off the wrong impression.

Their trio joined them for the movie as well. Again, Sawyer tried to pay for Ivy. Her face was red with frustration as she refused and made her way over to where Eva and Amy were standing. While they were standing in line, Quinn was chatting with Roman about his line of work. Somehow, they had broached the subject of his bathroom remodeling project, and Quinn was "interested in tips." It sounded more like he just wanted to hire Roman to come and finish the job.

"I'm kind of lost as to where to go next," Quinn was saying. "Maybe if you're not too busy, you can stop by and see where I went wrong. I'll pay you for your time. Have you considered doing any side work on your own?"

"We're actually in the beginning steps of starting our own business…" Max started, but Roman elbowed him.

"You are?" Sawyer wondered, and Ivy's ears perked up.

"It's all new." Roman eyed Max, who shrugged his shoulders as if to say, "People are going to find out."

"That's great!" Sawyer told him.

"Nothing is official," Roman said, looking nervous. "We work for a great company, and I have learned a lot from Roger, the owner. He's like family. Before we do anything, we want to leave in the right way."

"Say no more," Quinn told him. "I won't say a word. I know Roger. He's a good guy, but I have heard he's retiring soon. When you guys are ready, just give me a shout. If Roger taught you, then I know you'll do a great job at whatever you do. I'd be happy to work with you."

"Thank you." Quinn shook Roman and Max's hands.

When they were finally let into the theater, Ivy found herself between Roman and Sawyer once again. It didn't make her feel as uncomfortable as she thought it would. The seats were much roomier. She could still smell the scent of Roman's leather jacket every time he moved.

Sawyer offered to get them a drink after they had been sitting there for a while. Ivy gave him a five for hers. She had to make it clear to everyone that this was not a date. They were friends hanging out.

"So, are you enjoying your date?" Roman leaned over and whispered.

"Oh, my...God. Shut up!" She punched him. "How long have you been dying to say that?"

He snickered in his seat, her hit not affecting him. Ivy wished she could say the same for her knuckles. The man was solid muscle.

"So, do you think he knows it's not a date?" He couldn't help but laugh.

"If my knuckles weren't throbbing, I'd hit you again," she said to which he laughed once more.

"Do you want me to hold your hand during the movie so he understands?" He continued to snicker.

"You're hilarious." She rolled her eyes, but the thought made her insides flip. "Sawyer and I are not on a date. We are only friends. He's just really thoughtful. Besides, I don't think your date would like that too much."

"Eva is not my date," Roman corrected her with a laugh. "She's my cousin."

"Oh," it all became clear to her, "The green eyes."

"What?" he asked.

"Your eyes," she explained. "You have very distinct green eyes. So does Harper. I should've known you were related when I saw her eyes. She's beautiful, too."

"So, her green eyes and good looks should have made it clear we're related?" He was teasing her. "So, you think I'm good looking?"

Ivy was wondering where this flirting was coming from. Roman had been polite to her, but that was it. He was cold as ice the last time she had seen him. Then, she hadn't seen him in about a week. Now, he was Mr. Sex Appeal.

"Don't get a big head, Belmonte." She tried to act cool, but she had, once again, put her foot in her mouth.

"Eva is on a date with Max," he explained. "I'm the third wheel."

"Max landed your smoking hot cousin?" she wondered.

They seemed like such an odd pair. Max seemed like a sweet guy and he was cute in that smart, nerdy guy kind of way. He was gangly and a bit of a geek. She couldn't say much with her Darth Vader sweater, but with Eva's movie star looks, she didn't think she would give Max the time of day.

"Max is a good guy." Roman shrugged. "He's been working up the courage to ask her out for years. When she came home this time, he finally did and she said yes. They've been out a few times and it seems to be going well. And, as they say, love is blind."

"That serious, huh?" Ivy looked at him.

"Seems to be." He shrugged.

"And you're starting a business with him?" she questioned.

"Yeah, I guess we are," he told her, that nervous look returning. "It was only a conversation about a year ago. Now, I guess we're going to really do it. Roger is a great man to work for, but he was old when I started working for him fifteen years ago. What Quinn said is true; he's going to retire soon, and his son is going to take over. I'm not working for that spoiled man-child."

"I see," Ivy said. "I think that's great, Roman. That's a big step. Congratulations."

"Thanks, Ivy." He smiled at her.

His smile was dazzling, and it looked as though he was truly happy, but she couldn't shake the way she had seen him the last time. He was so robotic, as if he were on autopilot.

"Are you okay?" she couldn't help but ask him.

"Yeah," he laughed. "Why wouldn't I be?"

"I don't know," she shrugged, "The last time I saw you, you seemed...not yourself. I just wanted...I just hope you're alright, that's all. And I hope I didn't do anything to make you feel upset."

Something shifted in his eyes. His smile faltered for a split second. Ivy saw it. She wasn't sure if he noticed that she did. Ivy knew a mask when she saw it. She wondered if he was going to lie to her. When people saw through her cracks, when she was tired, that's what she did. She lied.

"I was having an off day," he said honestly. "Sorry if I was rude. I'm okay today."

I'm okay today. Ivy knew what that meant. She gently touched his arm, hoping he realized it was her way of saying she understood and he didn't have to try to explain. He smiled at her, the screen light reflecting in those green eyes like diamonds. There was a little jolt in her stomach. The longer he stared, the more she wanted him to.

"Here's your drink." Sawyer handed her the beverage, and Ivy removed her hand from Roman's arm.

The spell was broken. She gratefully took the drink, glad for something to distract her from whatever was going on with her nervous insides.

The movie they watched was actually pretty decent. It had the normal jump scares, but also a great plot and some genuine horror. There were a few moments when Ivy actually cringed and looked away.

Each time she did, she looked toward Roman. He would always be looking back at her. When the movie was over, they had a very passionate debate on their way back to the cars.

"This is a way better adaptation than the 90's made-for-TV miniseries," Ivy exclaimed.

"No way!" Max argued. "The casting choices were all wrong. Chris Evans? Really?"

"What's wrong with Chris Evans?" Roman asked. "He's Captain America!"

"Max is jealous because I think he's hot," Eva teased.

"He is hot!" Ivy agreed, fanning herself. "Especially with the beard!"

"Yeah, he is pretty hot," Roman chimed in.

"Roman, not you, too?" Max lamented.

"I call it like I see it." He shrugged his shoulders.

Max sighed, causing the rest of them to laugh. Ivy walked next to Eva, the two of them in conversation about how good the movie was.

"You're fun," Eva stated suddenly, making her think of Harper with her abrupt interjections. "You should come to game night."

"Game night?" Eva looped her arm through Ivy's.

"Yep, we play board games, eat, and let the kids run wild," she explained. "They're throwing a special one just for me since I'm in town. Ro, shouldn't Ivy come to game night?"

"Yeah, you'd have a blast," he agreed, nodding.

Ivy watched him to see if Eva inviting her over bothered him. He didn't seem upset, but she wasn't sure.

"Here, I'll look you up on Facebook and message you the details." Eva got out her phone.

"Oh, I'm not on Facebook," she admitted.

"What? Seriously?" Eva wondered.

"Yeah, just not my thing." She would not admit she was doing everything possible to avoid her mother.

"That's cool, girl," Eva said to her. "I respect that. Social media can be toxic. If it weren't for trying to stay relevant on stage, I probably wouldn't have one either. It is the way these days. Give me your number and we'll text."

Ivy did and was keenly aware of Roman staring her down. A lot of people looked at her oddly when she told them she didn't have a social media presence. She was glad Eva understood.

"Are you ready, Ivy?" Sawyer asked.

"Um, yeah," she said, even though she wasn't. "Bye, guys."

Eva hugged her. She didn't want to go at all. Glancing back, she caught eyes with Roman. He waved, and she felt that pull once again.

Chapter 6

Ivy woke to her phone buzzing. She had been so deep in the most bizarre dream about a zombie apocalypse that it took her a moment to understand where she was. After her head cleared slightly, she rolled over and saw her annoying phone was the culprit of waking her an hour before her alarm was set to go off. Even on the weekends she liked getting up in time to exercise and take Apollo for a walk, but when she wanted to, not before.

Her phone buzzed again, and she picked it up to see she had several text messages from Deacon, Eva, and Sawyer.

I had such a good time the other night! We should do it again soon. Maybe Carrie and Darren will be able to make it next time. Tell them they were missed! - Sawyer

See, Sawyer was just a friend and nothing more. He wanted to hang out with the entire library crew, not just her.

Game night. This weekend. 6PM. Bring any game you want to play. We might have it though. We're going to have so much FUN! - Eva

Ivy smiled. The thought of spending more time with the Belmontes made her happy. Plus, Eva was outstanding, so she knew it was bound to be a good time. Ivy sent her a text back and said she'd be there. She told Sawyer they would get something scheduled for the group.

Her phone buzzed once more, and this time Deacon was calling her.

"Yes?" Ivy answered, rolling her eyes.

"Finally," he breathed. "You need to put on your Sunday best. I'm on my way to your house. Butch wants to meet you after church. He would like for us to have lunch with him and his wife at their home."

"Seriously?" Ivy sighed. "It's Sunday, Deacon."

"Exactly, which is why we're going to church," Deacon responded. "Butch's church to be exact."

"I have my own church," Ivy whined. "And a good Christian woman, such as myself, should not be working on the Sabbath."

"It's not working; it's lunch," Deacon told her. She could hear a smile in his voice. "And I know you're not as innocent as you claim, Newton."

"Shut up." Ivy finally sat up, annoyed. "Why can't he meet on a business day like a normal person?"

"You'll learn today that Butch is anything but normal," Deacon laughed. "Now get dressed. I'll be there in ten."

Ivy groaned. She had zero interest in meeting Butch today. There were so many things she had planned to catch up on around her house. She seriously needed to do laundry. It was highly likely that she was down to one clean pair of underwear. Furniture needed dusting and floors mopped. It would apparently have to wait longer. Good way to highjack her Sunday, Butch.

She knew she shouldn't be so bitter. This was a great opportunity for the library. With that thought, she was a little more appreciative. That didn't mean she was going to go easy on Deacon.

He pulled into her driveway a short while later. Ivy got into his polished, very expensive sports car and they were off. She yawned and took another sip of her coffee.

"Did you not sleep well?" he asked.

"I didn't get home until around 1:00 and then you woke me up early." She yawned again.

"Where were you?" he wondered.

"I went to see a movie with Sawyer and a few other people," she explained. "No, we aren't dating."

"I didn't ask." He cut his eyes at her.

"Well, just making sure that's clear to everyone." She felt anger, or maybe just irritation, rise in her chest.

"Okay, you're touchy about this," he pointed out.

"Everyone thought we were on a date last night," Ivy blurted. "He tried to pay for everything, and I know it's because Sawyer is just thoughtful, but everyone else was getting the wrong impression. It was annoying and embarrassing. Roman teased me about it and…"

"Roman? Belmonte?" Deacon asked.

"Yeah, he was there with his cousin and Max," Ivy said. "A few others. Anyway, it was just…irritating."

"Clearly." He glanced at her.

"I'm going to have to clear the air with everyone," Ivy sighed.

"Well, to be honest, it's not anyone's business, Ivy," he said, and Ivy rolled her eyes at him. "What? Let them think what they want to. People need to mind their own business."

"Not likely in this town." She looked out the window.

"Why were you embarrassed?" he asked.

"I just didn't want anyone thinking we were dating." Ivy shrugged.

"Or you didn't want someone in particular thinking you were dating anyone?" he asked.

"What? What do you mean?" she asked.

"Which one is it?" he asked, slightly grinning. "It can't be Max, he's head over heels for Eva, always has been. All the others are taken, and you aren't that kind of woman. So, it has to be Roman. You didn't want Roman thinking you weren't available."

"Don't be ridiculous," she said and shifted slightly in her seat, the leather making her legs hot.

Ivy didn't want to discuss this anymore. She wasn't even sure why she'd opened up to Deacon this way. They were far from friends. Perhaps it was because they had history, or she was just really stupid from lack of sleep.

Deacon pulled into the mega-church's parking lot, and after being directed to a parking spot by one of the church's many volunteers, they climbed out to a rather chilly morning. There had to be over a hundred cars in the lot they were in. It was like a parking lot for an amusement park.

They followed the long line of churchgoers, dressed to impress the Lord, or rather each other, with their tailored suits and high dollar purses.

When she entered the building, greeters bombarded her with offers of coffee, doughnuts, and today's program. She felt overwhelmed by their eagerness to please, and she nervously hurried past them.

Deacon led her into the sanctuary. It was packed. There didn't seem to be a seat that wasn't occupied. The pulpit and stage area looked as big as the entire church she attended in Sparrows Ridge. The choir loft could easily hold 100 to 200 choir members.

"How many people go here?" Ivy asked.

"I'm not sure," he answered, looking for a seat amongst the bustling church. "I think it can hold 10,000."

Ivy believed it. She wasn't knocking anyone, but this just wasn't for her. She'd stick to the small crowds. It wasn't that she was overly religious, but her dad had taken her to church every Sunday while he was alive. And, surprisingly, he wasn't religious either. He'd said his faith was important to him; he believed in the Almighty, but he was far from Christian, as in "Christ Like." He'd told Ivy all they could do was love people and do good things. She tried to remember that.

The service was nice. The mega-church preacher didn't seem like the fraud she was expecting, and his message was the norm: "Love God, don't sin."

After the invitational song and prayer was over, Deacon and Ivy made their way through the crowd and stopped in front of a lovely older couple.

The man was well-dressed; his white hair was cleanly cut and was in stark contrast to his warm, dark brown skin. He had endearing brown eyes and a dazzling smile. His wife was a wisp of a woman, but there was strength in her large brown eyes. Her features were sharp, and she stood like a queen. Still, there was a kindness about her.

"Butch, how are you?" Deacon shook the man's hand. "Elaine, you look lovely as ever."

"We're in church, Deacon," Elaine deadpanned. "Keep it in your pants."

Ivy's eyes widened. Her jaw was probably at her knees as she looked at the older woman. There were many responses Ivy had expected from her, but that was not one of them. The three of them burst out laughing, watching Ivy's face go from pale to red.

"She's always been a kidder," Butch laughed. "Although vulgar from time to time."

"You enjoy it." Elaine smiled. "I didn't mean to mortify you, dear," Elaine said to Ivy.

"Oh," Ivy sort of laughed, "No, oh, it's fine."

"You're sweet, I can tell," Elaine said, taking Ivy by the arm and leading her toward the exit. "We're going to have to loosen you up a bit. Come, I see a mimosa or two in our future. I'm Elaine, by the way."

A short while later, Ivy was sitting in the home of Butch and Elaine Forrester, their very grand and expensive home. The kind of home with hardwood floors imported from Spain and chandeliers with Tiffany diamonds.

Ivy was admiring the ornately built-in bookshelves from her seat in a genuine leather armchair. She couldn't help but think about how Roman, with his love of building, would appreciate the detail. She would have to tell him about it when she saw him again.

"Here you are." Elaine brought Ivy a fruity-looking cocktail in a crystal glass. "I'm not a mixologist, but these are my specialties."

"Oh, wow!" Ivy exclaimed after taking a sip. "This is delicious."

"Told you," Elaine winked. "Now don't let my cocktail-making-skills fool you, Ivy. I am a woman of many talents. One of which is spotting a golden opportunity when I see it."

Elaine seemed to have said all of that in one quick breath. She was a very intimidating woman. Ivy wasn't sure if she worked or spent her days shopping, but she could definitely command a boardroom if she wanted, or any room for that matter.

"I want you to know something," she continued. "I think your library expansion is needed and a marvelous idea. When Deacon brought your proposal to Butch, I was floored by how much work you had done. You truly love what you do."

"Yes, I really do," Ivy said to her.

"Butch just couldn't say no." Elaine smiled.

"Don't let her fool you, Ivy," Butch and Deacon came into the room. "I'm sure Deacon has told you about my political endeavors, so Elaine thinks helping fund a library would look good for me. I have been so busy that I didn't even have time to look at your proposal. Elaine is the one that forced me to sit down and then made me choose it as our yearly fundraiser. She just wants everyone to think it was all my idea."

Ivy looked at her and Elaine shrugged. "I am not the type of woman who will let anyone railroad her, Ivy, but I am a very smart woman. I know this will look good for Butch. And he's a good man, better than most of those mouth-breathers in our local government. So, if you don't mind us using sprucing up your library in an effort to get Butch elected?"

"I would sell my left kidney to help this library." Ivy laughed. "I would normally feel odd about something like this, but I appreciate how forward you're being with your intentions. And, if it helps the library, I'm in."

Ivy spent the rest of the afternoon just enjoying herself. The Forresters were actually pleasant people. She hadn't thought she would find any common ground with them. They were from completely different worlds. Elaine came from a family of lawyers and doctors. Her mother was actually the first African American woman to become a doctor in her town back home in Indiana. Butch had made his fortune by starting a tech business that developed software for satellites and then sold it for millions at the right time.

He still had a desire for work so that's when he'd helped co-found Youling. He was nearing his retirement there and wanted to venture into local government. They had no children and spent most of their time and money on helping their community. It was hard to believe that there were really people out there that were honest to God philanthropists.

Butch really seemed to be a good man. He was stern, and Ivy could tell how he had run a successful business. He didn't mince words about how he wanted the fundraiser to go. He laid out all the details and wanted her approval on everything.

"All I need now is for you to promise me you'll be there," Butch said.

"Of course, as long as I don't have to pay for a plate. I'm pretty sure that's my entire paycheck for a month," she joked, but she wasn't lying.

"You're funny." Butch beamed at her like she was his long-lost daughter. "You'll be our guest of honor. Please, bring your staff with you and have each of you bring a guest. And, I was hoping you would say a few words, to encourage donors."

"You can count on it," she told him. "Thank you both so much. I know the citizens of Sparrows Ridge will appreciate this more than you know."

"Deacon, if you haven't snagged this one up by now, what are you waiting for?" Butch clapped him on the back.

Deacon's eyes shot to her, and he had the decency to look a little ashamed. Ivy sat there smugly as if to say, "Yeah, you missed out, buddy!"

"Oh, please." Elaine smirked. "We all know Ivy is way too good for the likes of you, you Tom Cat."

"You're not wrong there," Deacon agreed.

He was quiet on the way back, but probably due in part to Ivy talking most of the time. She was excited about the upcoming fundraiser and a little tipsy from Elaine's cocktails. When they got back to her house, Ivy was practically jumping out of her skin with excitement.

They were climbing the porch steps, Ivy still babbling about the fundraiser. She turned to look at him and before she knew it, he had closed the distance between them and pressed his lips to hers.

She was so shocked that she just stood there for a moment. Deacon wrapped his arms around her, deepening the kiss, his tongue finding its way into her mouth. It felt nice and his lips were familiar. Ivy could feel herself wanting to get lost in his embrace, but she had been down this road.

She pulled away from him. "Deacon."

"I messed up," Deacon said, his lips red from their kiss. "I messed up, and I'm sorry. I'm sorry I betrayed you. I'm sorry I hurt you. Elaine was right, I don't deserve you, but...I wish I did."

"Deacon," Ivy wasn't sure what to do or say. "It's in the past."

"I know you hate me and that kills me, Ivy." His eyes were so full of pain.

"I don't...hate you," she tried reassuring him, her hand still on his chest. "That's such a strong word. I don't have the emotional capacity to hate you, you should know that."

"You should, I'm an ass," he admitted.

"Well, that's true." She smiled and nudged his chin with her knuckle, and he looked at her. "But I can't do this. I can't."

"I know there is no going back," he said seriously. "But I still had to try."

"Well, you get an A for effort," Ivy told him, her lips still throbbing.

"Can we at least be friends? Like, when you see me in public, can you not run the other way? Will you...will you go the fundraiser with me?"

Ivy stared at him for a while. He looked pitiful, and her heart broke for him. Still, Deacon had really led her on. She wasn't going to go out with him just because she felt bad for him.

"I don't think that's a good idea, Deacon," she said. "But I will be your friend. I promise not to avoid you like the plague anymore, but I can't go out with you, not like that."

He smiled. "I can live with that."

Ivy eased out of his grasp and leaned against her door. Deacon smiled at her, his eyes still searching her face for a moment. Then, he turned and got back into his car and drove away.

Ivy sighed, not understanding what the hell had just happened, and let herself inside.

The first thing she noticed was the sound. Then, as she stepped forward, trying to determine what was making such a racket, her feet sloshed on a soaked carpet.

"What the hell?" she called, jumping back.

Apollo came bounding forward, his paws soaked. That's when Ivy recognized the sound: water, gushing water. It was coming from the hall bathroom.

"Oh, no!"

She went running forward and burst into the bathroom, slipping on the wet tile. She landed butt first in the cold water. Her elbow caught the sink on the way down, pain shooting up her arm, and she could almost swear she broke it.

"Son of a—mmmmm!" She bit her tongue.

Jumping to her feet and cradling her throbbing elbow, she looked for the source of the water. There, it was coming from behind the toilet. Sheetrock had already crumbled away from some areas as the water rushed out of a pipe in the wall.

"No!" she cried again.

Ivy ran out back, Apollo on her heels. She barely registered the cold air as she located the main water source. Ivy quickly turned off the water and stood there for a moment, catching her breath.

Coldness crept up the back of her legs, and she realized she was standing there in a dripping wet dress. Apollo had run off to do his business, completely unaware of her current turmoil.

"Thanks, bud." She shivered as she hurried back inside.

She assessed the damage once back indoors and wanted to cry. Not only was there a colossal mess of drywall on the bathroom floor, but the hall and part of the living room carpet were drenched. Unless the cleaning crew were miracle workers, it would have to be replaced. She had been planning to run hardwood floors through the entire bottom floor of the house, but she hadn't saved up enough money yet. She sighed, picked up her phone, and called her insurance agent.

Briefly, she had considered not getting homeowner's insurance; she really couldn't afford it. If it weren't for the little bit of money her father had left her, she wouldn't have been able to. So, she had decided to do the adult thing and add it to her expenses. At this moment in time, she was thankful for being responsible and sent a kiss above to her dad.

Keith Abernathy, her insurance agent, showed up with a cleaning crew around forty-five minutes later. Ivy had never seen a more glorious sight in her life. Having service like this was one of the many pros of living in a small town. No one minded house calls.

Keith was 70 years old but looked 105. Of course, Ivy would never tell him that. Though far from bald, he had thin white hair, big droopy ears, and a very prominent nose. He knew it, too. He told anyone who would listen that it was his best feature. An odd-looking man, but the heart of a saint.

He had been married to the same woman for over forty years. They had seven children together, all of which had graduated college and had families of their own.

He had once shown her a picture of his fifteen grandchildren, fourteen boys and one baby girl.

Ivy couldn't imagine a family that large. His wife, Kate, had stayed home and raised her children, while she worked from home as a pretty successful author of mystery novels. She still wrote and babysat many of her grandchildren. She was a frequent patron and advocate of the library. Ivy would have to tell her about the fundraiser.

"Oh, Ivy, I am truly sorry this has happened," Keith said, patting her hand as they stood in the kitchen, the clean-up crew already at work.

Ivy had changed into a pair of jeans and an old sweatshirt, along with a pair of rain boots. Keith had come prepared with a pair of his own.

"Thanks, Keith," she said. "I'd offer you some coffee, but we don't have any water at the moment."

"I'm fine, don't worry." He put his briefcase on the kitchen island and got to work.

After they had gone through all the paperwork and details, Keith had left her with what her next steps would be, like where she was going to stay until all the work was complete.

"Hey, Carrie. Yeah, it's me," Ivy said. "So, do you feel like being roomies for a few days?"

Chapter 7

Carrie was more than accommodating to Ivy and Apollo. Though Apollo had to spend a lot of time in the back bedroom; Carrie's apartment was small, and she was allergic to dogs.

"I'm so sorry," Ivy said when Carrie had another sneeze attack. "Let me take him for a walk."

Carrie lived a block from the library. Her apartment was in a tiny building that could house four tenants, which made her living area claustrophobic for Ivy. She was used to the openness and many rooms of her home. The old farmhouse was so spacious, she had forgotten what apartment life was like.

The January sky was gray with heavy clouds. It was brisk, but not overly cold. The chilly rain had subsided, which the residents of Sparrows Ridge were thankful for. Perhaps the Spring Fling the town hosted would be dry, unlike last year.

Ivy was still getting used to Southern weather and humidity. Back home, the ground would be covered in snow this time of year. She loved those warmer days, but sometimes she missed a good snow. Still, she prayed the weather continued to improve as the days went on. Every spring she took her homeschool book club kids to the county fair if they reached their reading goals. They normally did, but she was sure she would take them anyway, even if they didn't.

As Ivy was admiring the spring lilies that were fighting to bloom, she heard a vehicle turn down the road behind her. She moved herself and Apollo closer to the curb. This section of road was void of anything resembling a sidewalk.

"What are you doing in my neighborhood?" That deep timber echoed through her body.

She turned and saw Roman and Max sitting in the idling truck. They were dressed in work attire, clearly coming back from the job site. Roman was in the driver's seat, his muscular forearm stretched forward, his hand resting on the steering wheel. He wore a green flannel shirt, the thermal undershirt peeking out at the sleeves. Ivy couldn't deny that he looked good in green.

"Hey!" Ivy smiled widely. It came so easily to her when he was around. "I forgot you lived down this street. You would not believe the day I've had."

Ivy told them about what she was calling "The Great Flood."

"Is it that bad?" Roman looked concerned.

"The carpet is unsalvageable, and the bathroom wall is shot." She sighed. "It's been needing work, anyway. I'm surprised I didn't break the sink on my way down, not my most graceful moment."

Max and Roman laughed with her.

"Are you alright?" Roman asked.

"Yeah, it's sore and I'm sure it'll bruise, but it's no big deal." She scratched Apollo's head.

"Well, hopefully the repairs aren't that bad, and the insurance covers it all," he told her.

"Hey, I'll tell my insurance agent to use your business for repairs!" The thought hit Ivy suddenly.

"Yeah, tell him to send it to the office," Roman told her. "I'm sure Roger can send out a crew pretty quickly."

"No, I mean the business you and Max are starting," Ivy said. "I mean, if you're ready for something like that."

"We just finalized that paperwork yesterday," Max said proudly.

"You want to use us, for sure?" Roman asked her.

"Yeah, I mean, I've seen your work," she smiled. "I trust you."

"Thank you, Ivy." He suddenly looked a bit shy. "I can get out there tomorrow and then give a quote to your agent. I'm sure we could give you a good deal."

"Please do," she laughed. "If you have a discount for poor librarians, I'll take it."

They laughed at her attempt at humor.

"I better get back to Carrie's," she told them. "It's getting dark."

"Do you need a ride?" he offered.

"Nah." Ivy shrugged. "We'll take our time. Carrie is an angel. She's very allergic to dogs, so we'll give her nose a break for a bit longer."

"Ivy, I have a huge backyard that's fenced in," he told her. "Apollo could stay with us."

"I couldn't put that on you," she said, looking down at Apollo. "He's high maintenance."

"It'll be fine," Roman laughed. "Harper would love it. And, uh...well, we have a guest room. You're more than welcome to stay with us. Eva is there, too, so you wouldn't be the only female, uh, there."

Ivy felt her face go red. Had Roman Belmonte seriously just invited her, nervously she might add, to stay at his house? She looked at his face, then at Max, who was stifling a smile. Ivy was sure he was thoroughly enjoying himself.

"Just think about it." Roman smiled.

"Yeah, okay, thanks," she told him.

Roman waved and pulled away from the curb. She swore she saw Roman punch Max's arm as they drove down the road.

Ivy arrived back at Carrie's and told her about the exchange between herself and Roman.

"Are you going to?" Carrie asked, curiosity dancing in her eyes.

"Stay at his place?" Carrie nodded. "Are you crazy? I am not staying at Roman Belmonte's house."

"Are you scared?" Carrie teased as she held her cup of tea close to her body, curled up on the couch, a blanket over her legs.

"Of what?" Ivy asked from the seat across the room.

"Feelings," Carrie giggled like a teenage girl.

"There are no 'feelings,' Carrie." She rolled her eyes but could feel heat rising up her neck.

"Okay, sure," she snickered. "He's a nice guy, that's all I'm saying."

"It's usually the nice guys that are the worst," Ivy pointed out. "'Oh, I'm a nice guy; I've given you unwanted attention, but I'm nice so now you owe me sex.' It's disgusting."

"Men are pigs," Carrie said.

"That's an insult to pigs," Ivy laughed, and Carrie joined her.

"I guess they're not all bad." Carrie shrugged. "Look at Sawyer and Darren."

"Yeah, well, Darren is taken and not interested in us, or any other female," Ivy pointed out.

"True," Carrie sighed. "I want a marriage like what he and Jacob have. They're so dang good for each other. Still, they can't all be bad."

"Well, before you bring up Roman, I'm sure he has slept with both Stacy and Taylor at the diner," Ivy informed her. "You should have seen the lustful stares they gave him and the murderous glares they directed at me. He's not perfect."

"No one is," Carrie said, "And can you blame them for staring? He's dreamy."

Ivy didn't respond. She had more things to worry about than Roman being dreamy, even if she agreed.

As the week wore on, Carrie's allergies were getting worse. She swore she was fine and, "It would pass," but Ivy didn't believe her.

"I just sent Roman a text," she told Carrie. "He's letting me take him up on his offer to let Apollo stay at his place."

"And you?" Carrie teased.

"Funny." Ivy rolled her eyes as she walked back into her office.

She had received about fifteen different emails from Deacon with details regarding the fundraiser. Butch and Elaine were very thorough. It still amazed Ivy that they wanted her opinion on everything. Whether they took any of her suggestions was another story. She was also elated that the city and the Friends of the Library had accepted his offer to help. In fact, it thrilled them.

"Ivy, Sawyer is here to see you," Carrie said, poking her head through the door.

Ivy had been avoiding him. It was chicken of her to do so. She didn't want any of their friends to think anything of their movie adventure. What if they saw them together again. And why did it bother her so much?

Of course she told him about the fundraiser, but every time he had mentioned seeing her, she had said she was busy, which wasn't exactly a lie. Between her normal library programs and the fundraiser, she really had little time.

"Hello?" She stood up.

"Hey, Ivy," he said, smiling at Carrie as she left the office, his face red.

"Hey, sorry I've been so unavailable lately." She really did feel bad.

"No problem, I understand," he told her. "Hey, I wanted to ask you something."

They fell into an easy conversation about the fundraiser. She felt stupid for avoiding him. It wasn't his fault if people talked, and Ivy shouldn't sacrifice a good friendship to avoid town gossip. If she were being honest with herself, she knew why she didn't want people to think they were dating. Her conversation with Deacon came flooding back.

"Earth to Ivy," Carrie said from the door.

Sawyer was smiling at her as Carrie waved her arms, her bracelets jingling. They both laughed as Ivy came back to reality.

"What?" Ivy shook her head. "Sorry, lost in thought."

"Clearly," Carrie giggled in her cute little way.

"Can I steal Sawyer for a second?" Carrie asked both of them. "I need something from inside the storage room and I can't reach it."

"Are you using me for my tallness?" Sawyer pretended to be offended.

"I'll give you a piece of chocolate in return," Carrie offered.

"Then I am yours to do with as you please," he stood up.

Ivy noticed the look on Carrie's face as he walked toward her. She was nervous and a bit embarrassed. Sawyer clearly didn't realize what he'd just said or if he had, he did it on purpose to tease her.

"It's…um…the box of Valentine décor on the left-hand side," she stumbled over her words.

He nodded and headed toward the storage closet. As soon as he was out of earshot, Ivy burst into laughter. Carrie came rushing over to her, clutching her arm, and laughing with her.

"Holy smokes," Carrie giggled, wiping her eyes. "That was the hottest thing I have ever heard even if he did stick his foot in his mouth."

"How do you know what he said wasn't on purpose?" Ivy teased and Carrie's face went red hot. "Maybe you should go in there and see if he needs help."

"If I follow him in there right now, we might not be back for a few hours," she smirked, staring longingly in his direction.

"Carrie!" Ivy mocked at her indecency. "At the library? Scandalous!"

They laughed again, but quickly pulled themselves together as Sawyer made his way back. He sat the box on the circulation desk and Carrie went out there to greet him. The two of them chatted while Ivy watched. Carrie was clearly flustered at whatever Sawyer was saying and kept fiddling with her bracelets.

"Hey, Carrie," Ivy said as she approached the circulation desk. Carrie was checking in some books and looked up at them with a dazzling smile. Looking over at Sawyer, she thought he might pass out.

"Hey," she said.

"I'm leaving to get Apollo ready to head over to Roman's," she explained.

"Oh, okay," Carrie said and then looked at Sawyer.

"So, I'll see you two later." Ivy grinned and waved goodbye.

She wished Sawyer luck as she headed out the door. It was Friday, game night at the Belmonte's, and she was nervous.

He had come over and done an assessment of the repairs for her house. He was supposed to let her know if he could work within her insurance estimate soon. That was fine, but she couldn't get over how nervous she had been when he was there.

He had come alone. She had fully expected Max to be with him, but when she saw him pull into her driveway by himself, she felt her skin prickle with nervous energy.

The only thing they discussed were the repairs, but Ivy hadn't been able to keep her eyes off of him. She really had tried her best not to stare. It was next to impossible, though. She hoped he hadn't noticed or thought she was a weirdo.

After a quick shower, she grabbed the pie she'd made from the refrigerator, Apollo and his belongings, and headed out the door.

A short while later Ivy was knocking on Roman's door. She noticed all the cars in the driveway and was suddenly wondering if she should just go. She was sure there were more people here than she had expected, people she didn't know, and now she felt as if she were intruding.

Roman opened the door and greeted her with a smile. Noise seemed to explode from behind him. Children were running wild, multiple conversations floated about, and a game was blaring on the TV.

"Ivy." The way he said her name made her stomach flutter. "Come on in and join the chaos."

"Here, I made this for you…I mean, for you all." She handed him the pie as he ushered her inside. "Hopefully everyone likes chocolate cream pie."

"I like pie," Roman laughed.

"You brought Apollo?" Harper asked excitedly, running to greet her.

"I didn't tell him yet," Roman said.

"Tell me what?" Harper looked from his brother back to Ivy.

"Your brother has graciously agreed to keep Apollo for a while," Ivy told him.

"Really?" Harper jumped up and down. "Are you staying with us, too?"

"Just Apollo," she told him, and he looked a little let down.

"Well, this is outstanding news!" Harper said, smiling from ear to ear. "Can I take him with me outside, to the backyard?"

"Sure, introduce him to the other kids," Roman said after Ivy nodded her head.

Roman led her into the kitchen where food lined the countertops. There were dips, ribs, beans, chili, and an assortment of drinks. He placed Ivy's dessert next to a gorgeous white cake.

"I got you something," he told her.

"You did?" She raised her eyebrow.

He pulled open the refrigerator door and brought out a bowl. He took off the lid and there was a loaded Cobb salad inside. It was gorgeous and green with bright red cherry tomatoes, eggs, carrots, and all the other veggies she liked.

"Minus bacon," he told her. "I got you some fish, too."

"That's so thoughtful, Roman," she told him. "Thank you."

"No problem," he said and pulled out a few bottles of dressing. "I didn't know which kind you like, so I just got a bunch."

"I like them all," she laughed.

"You must be Ivy," an older woman with gray hair came into the kitchen.

She was wearing a soft blue dress and pink house shoes. Her thick, gray hair was pulled back in a loose braid. Ivy could imagine what her hair looked like when she was young. She was sure it was as full and beautiful as Roman's and Harper's.

"Ivy this my Tia Rita," Roman said and Ivy extended her hand. "She lives about an hour from here, but her and my cousin are visiting today and made most of the spread here."

"Oh, sweetheart, we hug here," she embraced Ivy and she found herself easing into the woman's hug.

"It's so nice to meet you," Ivy smiled. "Everything looks and smells so good."

"You'll have to try it all," Rita told her.

"My only experience with Mexican cuisine is the local restaurants," Ivy said sheepishly.

"Not to brag, but Tia makes the best food around," Roman hugged his aunt.

"Don't worry," Rita said to her, waving her hand. "I'll tell you what everything is and if you want you can try it."

"Oh, I know I want to try almost all of it," Ivy laughed. "If it tastes as good as it smells, I know it's going to be delicious."

"You are precious," Rita said to her.

"You're so sweet," Ivy laughed again.

"Ella es hermosa, Roman," Rita took Ivy's face in her hands. "You have kind eyes, a good soul."

"Oh, goodness. Thank you, Miss Rita," Ivy blushed.

"Call me Tia," Rita smiled and released her. "You are here with family."

Ivy felt her heart swell. She didn't know exactly why, but having Rita accept her so quickly was beautiful and made her nervousness about the evening fade.

"Come meet everyone," Roman said, opening the sliding door to the back patio.

Outside, Ivy found an oasis. The patio was warm and welcoming. An arched room covered the area with tall windows that were sure to let in copious amounts of natural light on a beautiful day. It was well-insulated because there was no chill, plus a large fire was burning in a stone fireplace in one corner.

Several comfy chairs were scattered here and there, but it was neat. A large farmhouse table was in the middle with people around it. Roman introduced her to the people she didn't know, most of his co-workers and their wives. There were a few there that were of the single crowd, two women and one man, who also worked with him.

They all seemed to know each other really well. Ivy felt awkward for just a moment, but it wasn't long before Eva put a drink in her hand and she was sitting next to the warm fire, chatting with the girls.

Ivy had friends; Carrie and Darren had hung out plenty of times. Still, she couldn't remember the last time she was surrounded by this many women having "girl talk." It was nice.

"Where are you from, Ivy?" Terri, one woman, asked. "You're not a southerner, that's for sure."

"That obvious?" she laughed.

"You don't have that drawl," Eva confirmed. "Although, I don't either. New York has beaten it out of me. I pick it up when I'm back here though."

"A majority of my youth was spent in Colorado, but I'm really from everywhere and nowhere," she said as honestly as she could. "My dad was in the military, so I moved around a lot."

"That explains it." Roman had walked up behind her, his voice making her jump. He smiled down at her. "Sorry."

"And what does that explain exactly?" Ivy cocked an eyebrow at him.

"Yeah, Ro, please elaborate." Eva eyed him with a smile.

"You're just…um…independent, strong-willed." He cleared his throat, noticing how all the women were staring at him. "It's…uh…refreshing. Anyone need a refill?"

"Food's done!" Max yelled from the grill, and the group headed inside to make their plates.

"Refreshing," Ivy heard Eva say to Roman.

"Shut up." Roman shoved her playfully.

Ivy watched them, wondering why Roman suddenly looked so embarrassed. She smiled at him when he noticed her watching. His face reddened, but he smiled back.

Ivy ate her fill and had a few more glasses of wine. Tia Rita had taken her by the hand and showed her all the food. She found out Ivy didn't eat meat and told her which ones to stay clear of. Ivy loved it all, the rice, the corn, the fresh homemade tortillas. She just wanted to take Rita home with her.

"You should have a restaurant!" Ivy said to her.

"Oh, my food is just for my family," Rita patted her hand. "But thank you. I'm so glad you liked it."

"Like it?" Ivy looked at her. "I wish I grew up eating this! I have been to a lot of places with a military dad, and trying new food was my favorite part. But this, it's just wonderful."

"Thank you," Rita smiled proudly. "I taught Roman a lot. He knows how to cook nearly all of this."

"And I'm pretty damn good at it," he bragged.

"Well, I'll just have to steal him when I have a craving." Ivy laughed and then blushed when she realized how it sounded.

"Yeah, you totally should do that!" Max snorted and Roman hurriedly left the table.

The group started up board games, which was a bloodbath. They had no problem tearing each other apart, and everyone was extremely competitive. It was good that Ivy was as well.

She, Roman, Eva, and Max had left a game of Uno to start Scrabble. Ivy won every round. Finally, Eva and Max surrendered, but Roman was determined to beat her.

"It's not going to happen, Ro," Eva told him.

They had amassed many onlookers with their last round.

"Yeah, give up, man," Max agreed. "She's a librarian. You're never going to win."

"Stranger things have happened," Roman argued, studying the board.

They were down to the last few remaining tiles. Roman had just played a thirty-point word and had two tiles remaining. He smiled, clearly thinking he had this won. Ivy thought it was possible. He had 302 points and she had 274, needing at least 28 points to win. It was going to be difficult. She wasn't sure if she had it or if she could play a word in the spaces left on the board.

It didn't help that she'd had another glass of wine right before this game. She was about to throw in the towel because the tiles were confusing her, but then she saw it.

"Oxygen," Ivy said out loud.

"We all need it," Max laughed.

"Shit!" Roman said as he saw it.

"Told ya." Eva clapped him on the back.

"Oxygen, 17 points, but 51 points on this triple word score." Ivy laid down the tiles. "And I'm out."

"The librarian is always going to beat you at Scrabble," Max laughed.

"Ivy! Come outside!" Harper called. "Percy is telling ghost stories."

"Chin up, Ro," Ivy said, grabbing her drink and heading for the door. "We can't all be winners."

"Oh, that's it." He jumped up and ran after her.

Ivy gave an embarrassing little squeak and ran outside. She felt like a teenager, running from the boy she had a crush on but secretly wanting him to catch her.

She didn't give in to her indulgence, as much as she wanted to. She quickly climbed into one of the comfy chairs with Harper. He curled up next to her, waiting for Percy to continue his tale of terror.

"You can't stay there forever," Roman threatened playfully.

She stuck her tongue out at him just as Harper said, "Ro, you're ruining the story!"

"Yeah, Ro, shh!" Ivy laughed.

Roman stared her down, his green eyes intense. She felt her face flush and as much as she wanted to blame the wine, she knew that would be a lie.

Ivy watched him out of the corner of her eye as he took a seat next to them. Apollo came bounding up, and Roman welcomed the big dog onto his lap. Roman's arm muscles flexed through his long-sleeved black shirt as he stroked the dog's head, listening to Percy's story.

Ivy tried not to let her imagination run wild. But here was a big manly man, who clearly loved his kid brother, and he was taking care of her fur baby. On top of all that, he was hot as hell and just downright sweet. He was considerate and treated her with compassion and equality.

What she originally thought was him treating her like a damsel was just him being kind. These qualities were making it really hard for her to look at him the way she should look at him, as a friend. Maybe she wanted to ruin their friendship.

Deep down, she wanted that. It wasn't hard wanting anything from him, emotionally or physically. She just wasn't sure if it was the best idea. They were friends and clearly something was there, but she had a feeling it had a lot to do with Harper.

The boy adored her. Of that, there was no doubt. The affection was definitely reciprocal. Harper was a doll, and she never wanted to do anything to hurt him. So, starting something with Roman could be problematic. And that was if he was even interested enough.

Harper laid his head on her shoulder, and Ivy wrapped her arms around him. Percy's story was good, but long, and Ivy could feel her eyes growing heavy. She remembered thinking she should probably head out soon, but then the next thing she knew, Roman was gently touching her shoulder.

"Ivy," he whispered.

"What? Oh, God, did I fall asleep?" She was now wide awake.

Harper was still wrapped in her arms, his steady shallow breaths an indicator he was sleeping as well.

"Yeah, you both passed out." Roman's smile dazzled even in the light of the dying fire.

"Sorry," she said, stifling a yawn.

"It's okay," he told her. "Let me get Harper in the bed."

"Where is everyone? Did I sleep that long?" She felt disoriented.

Roman picked Harper up in his powerful arms. Ivy noticed someone had draped a blanket over them.

"Everyone went home," he said. "Hang on, I'll be right back."

Ivy sat there, gathering her wits, while Roman took Harper inside. The poor kid must have been exhausted because he didn't wake up while Roman maneuvered him through the back door. She was slightly embarrassed. She stood and wiped her eyes, trying to brush away the remnants of sleep.

Making her way to the back door, Ivy folded the blanket. She laid it on the couch when she entered the living room. Apollo was curled up in his bed, next to the fireplace. It appeared he'd already made himself at home.

"Spoiled," she said to his sleeping form and realized how he seemed to just fit there.

Seeing her dog in Roman's living room wasn't strange at all. She wasn't sure how to take that.

"Well, he's out for the rest of the night," Roman said, coming down the stairs.

"I bet he's wore out," Ivy said. "They played hard."

"Those kids always do." Roman stood in front of her. "You must have been tired yourself." He laughed.

"Funny," she laughed. "It was from kicking your butt at Scrabble. That took a lot out of me."

"Oh, low blow." He smiled. "Leaving?"

"Yeah," she had her coat in her hands, "I need to get going. It's late."

"Are you sure you're okay to drive?" he asked her. "I have a spare bedroom. You're more than welcome to stay."

"I'm fine," Ivy told him. "I only had a couple glasses of wine."

"I don't know, Ivy." Roman's look of concern surprised her. "I'd hate for you to risk it. Max and Eva are staying. They're down in the basement. I'd feel better if you just stayed here."

"I'm okay, really," Ivy insisted. "Besides, Carrie lives like two seconds from here."

"Accidents happen two seconds from anywhere," he said sternly. "Say the alphabet backwards."

"What?" she laughed.

"Say it backwards and you can drive." He snatched her keys from her hands.

"Hey!" She reached for them, but he held them above his head. "That's not fair, you moose."

"Go on, recite," he commanded, a hint of a smile at the corner of his mouth.

"Z…Y…X…uh…" She was frustrated. "I couldn't do that on my best day."

She reached for the keys again, but he raised them higher. Ivy realized she was using his firm chest to push herself up to reach his hand.

"You work with books daily and kicked everyone's butt at Scrabble but can't recite the alphabet backwards?" he teased.

"No," she said, her cheeks turning red. "Now give me my keys before I resort to tickling you or something. You are in the perfect position right now."

"Wow, what a threat," he laughed.

"Roman," Ivy huffed like a little girl about to throw a tantrum.

"Ivy," he mimicked her tone.

He stared down at her, his green eyes seeming to look straight through her. She felt her stomach do a flip. She moved away from him and crossed her arms.

"You're being difficult," she finally said.

"No, I'm being responsible," he countered. "Touch your nose, first with one finger and then the other."

"Seriously?" She rolled her eyes.

"Yes, seriously," he said. "Do that without issue and I'll give you your keys. I promise."

Ivy stared at him for a moment, glaring. She was tired, but not drunk. Still, she realized this was the only way to have her keys returned to her. Sighing, Ivy took her right index finger and promptly poked herself in the eye.

"Son of a…" She blinked.

Her aim had been terribly off. Shocked, she looked at her treacherous finger and then at Roman. The punk had been right; she was still drunk, or slightly buzzed anyway.

He smiled down at her. "I'll show you to your room."

"Shut up." She followed him up the stairs.

Family photos, mostly of Roman, Harper, and Eva, lined the walls leading to the second floor. A plush light gray carpet with deep green embellishments ran down the middle of the staircase and continued into the hall as they reached the top.

Roman led Ivy to a nice-sized spare room with a queen bed. It had matching furniture and its own bathroom. A window, with a balcony seat, was draped with heavy blue curtains that matched the bedding and circular area rug. Ivy was impressed and a bit jealous that his house was better decorated than hers.

"Eva usually keeps a few extra pajamas in here for when she visits," Roman said, walking toward the dresser and pulling open the drawers. "And it's empty."

"It's okay," Ivy shrugged, "I can sleep in this."

"Hang on," he said, leaving the room.

He came back a few seconds later and handed Ivy a shirt. It was large, black, and had a rock band's logo she'd never heard of splashed across the front in white lettering.

"You can wear this…um…if you want," he said. "Uh, there is a spare toothbrush, toothpaste, all the essentials in the bathroom. Just make yourself at home."

"Thanks," Ivy told him.

Roman stood there for a moment, just looking at her. His eyes searched her face, and she almost swore they rested on her lips before he cleared his throat. Her heart pounded.

"You're welcome," he said. "Goodnight."

"Night," she called after him.

Ivy decided on the T-shirt. She told herself she could sleep in her jeans and sweater, and she probably could, but given the choice, she would sleep in anything else.

Maybe in Roman's arms, her thoughts whispered.

Her face blushed as she stood at the sink brushing her teeth. After washing her face of her makeup, Ivy settled into the overstuffed mattress. It seemed to envelop her, and she could feel her eyes growing heavy with sleep. Just as she was about to drift off, a horrible cry startled her. Harper.

She bolted out of bed and ran into the hallway. Finding his room by the sound of his sobs, Ivy burst through the door and ran to his bed.

Harper lay there, crying, shaking, calling out for someone, reaching for them. She grabbed his hands so he wouldn't hurt himself.

"Shh, Harper, it's okay." She held him to her chest just as Roman dashed into the room. "It's okay, baby, it's just a dream. It's just a dream."

Ivy could feel her heart shatter as the young boy clung to her, soaking the shoulder of her shirt with tears.

"Ivy," he cried. "Ivy."

"I'm here, sweet boy." She kissed the top of his head.

"Ro?" he cried more; his eyes still closed.

"I'm right here, buddy." Roman kneeled next to them and put a comforting hand on his baby brother. "You're safe, Harper. You can sleep."

Harper sniffled but was calmer. Ivy continued to rock him, smoothing his hair with her hand and rubbing his back. She wasn't sure how long she sat there—her and Roman—but eventually Harper drifted off into a quiet sleep.

Apollo eased his way into the room and curled himself next to the young boy. Harper seemed to sense him and rolled over, draping his arm over the big dog.

Ivy and Roman eased out of the room. Roman closed the door, and they walked silently back to Ivy's guest room.

"He gets night terrors sometimes," Roman explained when they stopped at her door. "His therapist says it's from…what happened. I'm sure you've heard."

"I'm so sorry, Roman." Ivy reached out and touched his arm.

Ivy knew he was referring to the rumors around town about his parents' murder. She had heard many things about it.

"I've heard all the rumors," he said.

"Roman, you don't have to explain anything to me," Ivy said to him.

"It's okay," he told her. "The truth is my parents were shitty people who put their kids in danger. I wanted to leave when I was eighteen, but I didn't because of Harper. He was only five years old. I couldn't leave him with them."

"Of course not," Ivy said.

"He was only nine when it happened," Roman looked down at his hands. "I was asleep when I heard the first few shots. I ran to Harper's room, but he wasn't there. I…found him downstairs. He had been shot in the back."

"Dear God." Ivy covered her mouth and felt a surge of anger run through her body.

"My parents had been killed in the living room." His hands were clenched into fists. "I called 911, and thankfully they got Harper to the hospital in time. The only reason I lived was because I had been sick that day. They didn't think I was home; thought I was at work."

"Are they in prison?" Ivy asked.

"Yeah, they're both doing life sentences," Roman said. "But that brings me no solace. I thank God every day that Harper pulled through. I just wish he didn't have to live like that, with the nightmares. I play it back in my head all the time. What if I had been faster, stronger? What if I had been braver? You know, stood up to my parents for bringing that kind of danger, their drugs, into our lives? I could have done something. I should have done something."

"Roman, you can't do that to yourself." Ivy stepped toward him, placing a hand on his arm. "I can't imagine what you've been through, and I will not insult you with the whole 'everything happens for a reason' crap. But it did happen, and it wasn't because of anything you did or didn't do."

He looked back up at her with a sad smile on his face. "Thank you, Ivy. I don't know why I dumped all of that on you. You're just…really easy to talk to."

"I am a pretty good listener if I say so myself." She winked.

That got a smile out of Roman. He suddenly stood up pin straight, looking down at her. Ivy's pulse quickened and she could feel herself drawn to him, to that look in his dark green eyes.

This was a bad idea, she told herself.

She hadn't been oblivious to the fact that Roman had been shirtless throughout their entire conversation. She would not pretend she hadn't stolen glances at his dark skin and broad shoulders or peeked at how a tiny trail of hair started at his naval and disappeared into his pajama bottoms.

It's just that there had been other things at the forefront of her mind. Right now, not so much. Now, the only thought she had was what it would be like to wrap her arms around his neck and press her lips to his. The way he looked at her made her wonder if he was having the same thoughts.

"I guess we should get some sleep," he said, his breath coming out roughly.

"Right." She cleared her throat, pulling at the hem of her shirt, noticing how his eyes lingered on her bare legs. "Um, goodnight." She opened her door.

"Ivy," he said, and she turned to look back at him. He had moved closer.

"Yeah?" She felt nervous.

"Thank you," Roman nearly whispered, and he was so close she could feel his words dance across her cheeks.

"Of course," she told him. "That's what friends are for."

She smiled and slipped into the room, shutting the door behind her. Ivy leaned against the door, settling her pounding heart.

That's what friends are for? Good one, Ivy.

It took every ounce of her willpower not to jerk the door open and throw herself into Roman's arms. Before she could completely embarrass herself, she crawled back into the bed. It took a very long time to fall asleep.

Chapter 8

Ivy awoke to the sound of rain hitting the windowsill. For a moment, she forgot where she was and sat up. A moment of panic flooded her system as she took in her surroundings.

Then she looked down at the rock T-shirt she was wearing and remembered she was at Roman's. She had slept in Roman's house, in his shirt that smelled like freshly washed sheets. Memories of their conversation late last night came swimming back to her.

She could recall words, laced with years of pain, see the despair in his emerald eyes as he recounted the incident that had shattered Harper's sense of security. Ivy had wanted to comfort him, but she knew if she moved any closer to him, she'd lose the tiny bit of control she had over her desires.

The way his body looked, stone hard and fit, was enough to make heat rise to her face. She had been so close to him. She could still feel the way his words brushed against her face, warm and inviting. Resisting the urge to reach out and touch his face, let her fingers work their way down, explore the powerful muscles of his neck and chest, it had almost been unbearable.

It wasn't the time. Roman had lost so much, and he was confiding in her; he wasn't asking her to jump his bones. When had she become such a garbage friend? In fairness, she had never been this attracted to one of her friends. It still didn't make it right to take advantage of their moments of vulnerability, no matter how much she liked their abs.

Sighing, she got out of bed and quickly dressed. Her lustful thoughts made her feel guilty and like an intruder in Roman's home. He had been so inviting, making sure she was safe, and here she was wondering what it would be like to have him hold her, kiss her, and more. Her plan was to slip out before anyone else awoke.

Rushing downstairs, she realized her plans were shot. Eva walked by, nodding at her with a cup of coffee in her hand.

"Want some?" she asked.

The coffee smelled divine, and she followed Eva to tell her thanks, but no thanks. She really needed to get out of here before she saw Roman. When she stepped into the kitchen, she saw the entire family was already there.

"There she is," Roman said to her as he cooked away at the stove. "Thought you were going to sleep all day."

He was wearing a white shirt and loose gray joggers that seemed to accentuate his ample legs and other areas. Ivy had to try hard not to stare like some creeper. He was frying bacon, cooking eggs, and had pancakes on a griddle. It smelled amazing, and Ivy could feel her stomach rumble in response.

"I considered it," Ivy replied honestly and took the cup that Eva handed her.

Eva patted the seat next to her and Ivy sat down, holding the warm cup in her icy hands.

"Ivy, I walked Apollo this morning and gave him his breakfast." Harper came up to her, a big smile on his face and Apollo at his heels.

The young boy looked vibrant, well-rested. There was no trace or evidence that the night terror he'd experienced had any effect on him. She wondered if he even recalled it taking place, or that she had rocked him back to sleep.

"Harper, you're the best." She ruffled the boy's hair.

Harper laughed and hugged her. Ivy welcomed his small body in her embrace and kissed him on the top of the head.

"Do you want to come to Mass with us?" he asked her. "Can she come, Ro?"

"That's up to Ivy," Roman said, his eyes darting to her momentarily. "But I don't think she's Catholic, Harp."

"Meh, who cares?" Eva shrugged, and Max nodded his head in agreement. "We welcome all. You should join us."

"I don't want to intrude on your worship," Ivy told them.

"You won't be," Roman told her. "Want some pancakes?"

In less than an hour Ivy had stopped by Carrie's, taken a quick shower, and threw on a long-sleeved black dress, black tights, and a pair of ankle boots. Carrie wasn't there for her to ask if she looked Catholic church appropriate, but she didn't think it was too bad.

Soon she was in the car with the Belmontes and Max, on the way to Mass. Harper was filling her in on how visitors should take part, or lack thereof, during the ceremony.

"You just can't take communion," Harper told her. "Only Catholics can do that. You'll just stay seated."

"Right, stay seated, got it." Ivy nodded.

"Harper, you're weirding her out," Roman said, laughing.

"No, it's fine," she smiled. "This is a learning experience. I find other religious practices interesting."

"Whoa, easy," Roman threw up one hand, keeping the other on the steering wheel. "We are not religious, just…have faith."

"I get that," Ivy nodded.

"I'm only coming because my hot girlfriend told me to," Max said from the backseat, sitting next to Eva.

"Who said I was your girlfriend?" She raised an eyebrow.

"Oh, I thought I told you," Max winked at her. "Surprise."

"For Pete's sake." Eva rolled her eyes, but she was smiling.

Ivy smiled back at them while she considered Roman's statement. She understood where they were coming from. Ivy had her own faith but didn't like being lumped in with the many people that shared her faith. Mainly because those who claimed to be filled with Christ's love were the worst people she'd ever met.

It wasn't long before they pulled into St. Vincent's Catholic Church. The building was tall, white-washed stone, with high towers and a cross at the top of the uppermost steeple. Stained glass windows adorned the outer walls, nearly reaching from the ground to the roof. Ivy saw two large wooden doors, stained with a cherry wood hue, and they were so big she could see them from the parking lot.

Ivy couldn't recall ever seeing this building, but that wasn't too surprising. St. Vincent's was in the next town over, and although it straddled the city line with Sparrows Ridge, she hadn't been out there often.

There were a lot more people than she thought would be here on a Saturday evening. Roman explained that they usually came to Mass on Saturdays and spent their Sundays at home.

"It's our lazy day," Harper said as they walked up the church steps.

"Our catch up the laundry day," Roman joked.

"Or Roman tinkers with his car all day and I have to order pizza for dinner day," Harper laughed. "Told you, it's his girlfriend. He needs a real one."

"Get up there with your cousin." He playfully shoved Harper forward to Eva as Ivy laughed.

Eva and Max led them into the church. They were greeted by who she assumed were church elders. The group dipped their fingers into the holy water and made the sign of the cross. Roman guided Ivy through it and explained it was their way of blessing themselves.

The rest of the service went as any other church service went. There were songs, greeting each other, the message which was about guarding your heart against the evils of the world, and then communion.

Ivy remained in her seat, as did Max and a few other visitors. Afterwards, they talked to the priest for a moment.

"You're new," he said to her after shaking Roman's hand.

"Just visiting," Ivy explained and shook his hand. "I'm Ivy Newton."

"I feel as if we have met. Have we?" Father Isbell asked her.

Ivy felt her face redden under his stare. She never enjoyed being the center of attention, and now their group was all looking at her.

"She's Sparrows Ridge's librarian," Roman explained.

"That must be it." He eyed her as if he were still trying to place her. "Ivy, ancient Greeks would give newlyweds an ivy wreath to symbolize their faithfulness to one another. It is derived from an old English word which means loyalty."

"Cool! What does my name mean?" Harper asked the priest.

"It means 'knucklehead,'" Roman told him. "Let's go eat. Father, thank you for your message."

The group left, and Ivy felt as if Father Isbell had seen straight into her past. Her mind automatically went to the incident with her stepfather, but she had been a minor and it was self-defense. She had gone through counseling, and they'd sealed her records. Besides, how could a Priest in "nobody's ever heard of it," USA know about her past? She was just paranoid.

Ivy brushed off her insecurities. She would not let the fear or pain of her past ruin a perfectly good day, especially when that day included hanging out with Roman.

After dinner, they all headed back to Roman's to watch a movie. It didn't take much convincing to get Ivy to agree. It was an action movie and while she enjoyed them, this particular film was over-the-top ridiculous, and Ivy had trouble keeping her eyes open.

Poor Harper didn't make it and had fallen asleep on her lap. Roman scooped him up and carried him to bed.

"Max, are you headed home? Can I catch a ride?" Ivy asked him.

"Yeah, but I'm in my work truck, Ivy, and it is literally piled with stuff," he told her apologetically. "You wouldn't fit unless you wanted to sit on top of a grimy toolbox."

"I'll give you a ride," Roman told her, coming down the stairs. "Max, will you stay here with Eva and Harper until I get back?"

"No problemo." Max kicked back on the couch.

"Bye, Ivy," Eva told her, hugging her tightly. "Please come hang out with us again before I go back to New York!"

"Sure." Ivy smiled and headed out the door with Roman. "Thank you, I should've driven myself over here after dinner," Ivy said as they climbed into Roman's car.

"I don't mind." He smiled at her.

Ivy felt heat rise from her chest and settle on her cheeks. Her fair skin always betrayed her emotions. She hoped the darkness hid her reaction from Roman. She didn't want him to know what just a smile could do to her.

Before she was ready, Roman pulled into Carrie's apartment complex.

"Thanks again," she said, reaching for the door handle.

"I could tell Father Isbell freaked you out," he said, making her turn and look at him. "I'm sorry about that. He can be pretty intense. He's ex-military and a former teacher for at-risk youths. Being sort of an interrogator comes naturally to him."

"Oh, no, it's fine," she waved her hands. "It wasn't just him. I'm naturally shut off. Shy, if you will. So it wasn't a good mix."

"You don't seem shy," he commented.

"Well, I feel like I know you guys so I'm more open, I guess," she laughed.

"Sort of," he remarked, putting the car in park.

"Sort of?" she wondered.

"Well," he started. "I know you, but I don't know anything about you."

"Of course you do," Ivy laughed nervously. "You know I'm superb at Scrabble."

"Funny." He grinned in spite of himself.

"See, now you know I'm funny." She grinned back.

"That's fine, keep your secrets." He smirked. "You'll tell me when you're ready."

"You know all there is to know." She shrugged.

"I know you're Ivy Newton, librarian, pescatarian, owner of Apollo," he responded. "I know nothing about what makes you who you are or anything prior to you becoming our town's librarian. You just appeared, came in on a western wind."

"You make me sound so mysterious." Ivy couldn't help but laugh.

"You are," he said, giving her that intense stare he was so good at.

"Perhaps," she said and got out of the car. She felt hot suddenly.

Roman got out with her. Ivy smiled as she realized he was walking her to the door.

"I'm a big girl, you know," she told him.

Carrie didn't seem to be home, so she pulled out the spare key she had given Ivy.

"Just wanted to be sure you're safe," he told her.

She turned, and he was so close to her. Ivy felt herself wanting to reach out and touch his chest, but she pushed her back against the door and kept her hands at her sides.

"I appreciate you letting me hang out with you guys this weekend," she said to him. "I've had a lot fun. Probably more fun than I've had in a long time."

"Me too," he told her. "Goodnight, Ivy."

Ivy did not know what came over her. In fact, it felt as though she was having an out-of-body experience. There was just something in the way he looked at her, or maybe in the way he wanted to know her better. Whatever it was, it fueled her bravery.

She reached up and hugged him. It was one of those full body, wrap your arms all the way around someone kind of hug. Ivy felt his strong arms circle her body as he returned her embrace. When she pulled back, his face was just right there, his breath on her lips.

Ivy panicked. Trying to explain why she was suddenly so afraid was difficult. Kissing him was all she had thought about for days. Now that he was right here in front of her, she didn't know how to go about doing this. What would it mean to their friendship? How would this affect Harper?

The thought made her pull away. Roman released her, and she looked down at her feet.

"Ivy?" he said, and his deep voice made her look up.

"Yeah?" she asked.

"I…" he started and searched her face for a moment.

Roman took her face in his hands and easily found her lips. His mouth was warm and soft. She wanted him, more than she had ever wanted anyone. She wrapped her arms around his neck, and he pressed into her. His body was pure heat, warming her from the inside out.

Ivy's mouth parted as his tongue gently but firmly pushed inside, tasting every bit of her. His hands ran down her back, and he pulled her closer to him. Her head was spinning as his kiss deepened. All too soon they pulled apart, breathing heavily.

"I… I shouldn't have done that."

"What?" She was confused, not sure she had heard him correctly.

He let go of her. His green eyes had a glazed look. Roman pushed a strand of her hair from her face.

"I can't stop thinking about you," he told her, but he said it like it was a curse, like it hurt him.

"Is…is that a bad thing?" she asked him.

"No," he said, putting his head down and then looking back up at her. "Yes."

"I'm so confused, Roman." Ivy felt her heart drop.

"I know," he ran his hands over his face. "And I'm so sorry. That's why I shouldn't have done that. I'm sorry. I'm messed up in here." He pointed at his chest. Ivy's heart dropped a little more. What was he trying to tell her?

"I…lost…someone," he told her finally. "My fiancée and my child."

Ivy couldn't hide the surprise on her face.

"It was right before you moved to town," he told her. "It was a car wreck. I…was driving. I haven't…dated…or wanted to…"

"Roman—" Ivy started.

"I'm so sorry, Ivy," he told her, not being able to look at her. "You made me feel something for the first time in a long time, and I thought…I want you so much, if you only knew, but…I'm not ready."

"It's okay, Roman," Ivy told him, but inside it shattered her. "I understand you're not ready. It's okay."

"Why are you so good?" he asked, looking at her finally.

"I'm not," she told him.

"You are." He was in pain, torn, and Ivy had something to do with that.

"Roman, you should go home," she told him.

"Right," he said, but he didn't move.

Ivy prayed he would leave, right now, right at this moment. He needed to get away from her because even though he believed she was good, she was selfish. She wanted to ignore his pain and pull him back to her, kiss him deeply, even if it hurt.

Finally, he nodded and shoved his hands in pockets, then walked back to his car. She hurriedly entered the apartment, shutting the door behind her with more force than she had intended. She had gone from the highest high to the lowest low faster than was healthy for any human being.

Covering her face with her hands, she slumped against the door with a shaky breath. She felt foolish, ashamed even. She felt like Roman had cheated on his dead fiancée with her just now. Still, she wished with all her heart that he would come back, knock on the door like some Rom-Com hero, and tell her he was wrong.

This wasn't a movie, and it definitely wasn't a fairytale. Roman wouldn't suddenly come walking in and sweep her off her feet as if she were a princess locked away in a tower. They wouldn't share a magical kiss in the rain and ride off on his valiant steed into the sunset.

In the real world, people hurt, they lived with trauma. Sometimes they could overcome it, and sometimes they couldn't. She knew firsthand what it was like to walk around with heavy baggage. It took her a long time to open up and trust, and the first time she had, she'd trusted a playboy like Deacon.

It was foolish of her to think this time would be any different. She wasn't mad at Roman. When she told him she understood, she'd meant it. That didn't mean she wasn't hurt.

Ivy wanted to apologize, but that meant seeing him again—and oh God, she had to see him again! She had to see him a lot!

He had her dog! He was going to be working on her house, more than likely. Ivy hurried to the bathroom. Maybe a nice shower would melt away the undeniable stain of humiliation and rejection that would surely follow her for the rest of her life.

Chapter 9

The next morning Ivy got up like the walking dead. She was full of groans and creaks, and she was sure she heard her neck snap in three places. Sleep had not found her quickly the night before and when she did finally close her eyes, the neighbors to the left had a full-on shouting match, followed by what Ivy assumed was amazing make-up sex.

"Have fun last night?" Carrie asked her as she walked into the living room.

Ivy jumped as she said, "Nothing happened."

"Um, that's not what I asked." Carrie eyed her suspiciously. "Unless something did happen…did it? Tell me!"

"How was your weekend?" Ivy dodged the question. "You weren't here when I got in."

"I had a date—I think." Carrie blushed.

"A date?" Ivy asked, sipping on her tea.

"With Sawyer," Carrie said. "Is that weird? I know I thought he was into you, but then he asked me to go for a walk after work and—"

"I think it's great, Carrie," Ivy said to her. "Sawyer is an amazing guy."

"You're not answering me by the way," she pointed out. "What happened?"

"I have to go walk Apollo," Ivy announced, grabbing her keys and walking out the door.

"You can't avoid me forever, Ivy Newton!" Carrie called after her.

Ivy was terrified the entire ride over to Roman's. If she could, she would avoid him for the rest of time, but she had a responsibility to Apollo. Why had she agreed to this?

When she pulled into Roman's driveway, he was in the garage loading up his work truck. Ivy felt her cheeks go red at the sight of him and the memory of his lips on hers.

Stupid cheeks! she thought.

Gathering her courage, she turned off the engine of her old truck and stepped out.

"Good morning," Roman greeted her.

"Morning." She nodded her head, not really looking at him.

"Want some coffee? I just made a pot," he offered.

"No, thank you." She tried politeness. "I'm just going to get Apollo's walk in. I need to get to work."

"Okay," Roman nodded. "He's inside with Harper."

Ivy smiled and walked toward the house. Harper and Apollo were excited to see her, one wagging his tail and the other ready with a warm hug.

"Can I go with you on Apollo's walk?" Harper asked.

"Sure, if it's okay with your brother," Ivy said, hearing Roman approach the kitchen.

"That's fine with me," he said, stopping beside Ivy.

She could sense his closeness. As much as she wanted to lean onto his strong shoulder, she took two steps away. Roman seemed to sense her purposely putting distance between them.

"I'll go grab my coat." Harper ran off, leaving them standing there alone.

Exactly what she'd wanted to avoid.

"You sure you don't want some coffee? You might need it to keep up with that one," Roman joked.

"I'm fine," Ivy told him as she fiddled with Apollo's leash.

"Don't trust my coffee making abilities?" he laughed.

"What? No." Ivy shook her head, feeling more uncomfortable by the second. "I'm more of a tea drinker, that's all."

"Well, now I know something else about the mysterious Ivy Newton," he said as he poured himself a cup of the hot brew.

The statement made Ivy's eyes shoot in his direction. He stood there, a steaming cup of coffee at his lips, staring at her as if she were the most interesting person he had ever met.

"It's not a very defining detail about a person," she said, shrugging.

"I think knowing someone's preferred beverage is very personal," he disagreed.

"Okay, Roman," Ivy said and resisted rolling her eyes, annoyed.

Was he flirting with her? After last night, she didn't think he would want anything to do with her, not in that way. She hooked Apollo to his leash and left the kitchen without another word.

This is what she did when someone got under her skin. She treated them with indifference. And Roman—he was deep under her skin.

Harper came down the stairs, coat on and ready to go for their walk.

"Let's go," he said, as if Ivy had been the one holding them up.

She couldn't help but laugh and followed him out of the house. She could feel Roman's eyes on her as she left with Harper down the street. Glancing back, she saw him leaning against the porch railing, watching them.

It made no sense to her as to why he would be remotely interested in knowing her. Maybe he was just curious by nature. Ivy would not deny that she wasn't very forthcoming with the details of her life prior to moving to Sparrows Ridge.

When people asked, she gave them watered down answers, just like she had done at the party. She was from nowhere. No, she had no family. She'd moved here to get away from the city life. Answers that could apply to anyone.

She had her reasons for her reserved answers, but it was none of their business. It definitely wasn't any of Roman's.

Ivy left quickly after bringing Harper and Apollo back. It looked as though Roman wanted to say something to her, but Ivy didn't give him a chance. For the next few days, she kept the same routine: walk Apollo every morning and afternoon (Harper would join her before he had to go to school), say only what was necessary to Roman, and go back to Carrie's.

On the fourth day, her successful strategy of avoiding Roman was shot. He came into the library during her book club session with her homeschool kids.

His dark hair was tousled in a way that shouldn't be humanly possible, and it really shouldn't have looked that good. The dark jeans he wore hung perfectly on his hips, and the checkered flannel shirt would have looked ridiculous on anyone but him.

The group of moms who were waiting on their kids looked up and watched him as he made his way through the library. Roman seemed oblivious to their lustful stares.

The kids noticed she was distracted and looked up to see where her attention had landed.

"Who is that?" Gemma Stewart asked, eyeing Roman with interest.

"A friend," Ivy stated. "Let me see what he needs."

"Holy cow, he's hot," Tiffany Walker grinned, and Gemma nodded her head in agreement.

"Girls," Ivy warned the two pre-teens. "You guys keep working on your arena project. I'll be right back."

"You go, Miss Ivy." Gemma gave her two thumbs up.

Good lord!

"Hey, sorry to interrupt," Roman said to her. "I got the go ahead from your insurance company, and I think I have an exceptional price on the repairs. I just need your signature on a few things. If I can get it faxed over before 5:00, I can actually start tomorrow."

"Really? That would be great." Ivy felt relieved. She was so ready to be back home. "Follow me to my office and we'll get everything signed. Darren, will you keep an eye on the younglings for me?"

"Sure thing." He smiled widely at both of them.

"Younglings?" Roman asked.

"They think it's funny." She smiled. "Pop culture references keep us on the same level most days."

Roman sat down in the chair opposite her. Ivy almost laughed at the look on his face. He seemed like a wild animal who had suddenly been caged. Roman wasn't made to sit behind a desk.

"This is a great price," Ivy said after looking at the paper. "A lot cheaper than what I've seen during my research on estimated costs. Are you sure you're not cutting yourself short?"

"I'm sure," Roman reassured her. "Newman, my supplier, is giving us a great discount for being exclusive with them. I can pass that down to my customers and still make a profit."

"Okay, I'll sign this as long as you're sure." Ivy would feel awful if she cheated anyone out of the pay they deserved, especially him.

"Don't worry," he smiled, making Ivy's heart jump. "I'm sure."

Ivy quickly looked away from him and signed the contract. She stood a little too fast and handed him the paper. It was more like shoving it in his face, but she tried not to think too much about it.

She felt awkward in most social settings. It's not that she couldn't handle herself well; it just took a lot of concentration not to put her foot in her mouth. She had a habit of saying exactly what she was thinking. And to be honest, being social was draining. Anyone who said differently was a psychopath, in her opinion.

With Roman, it was different. Or at least it had been. She wanted to talk to him, to interact. Feeling completely at ease with someone was rare for her, but she had felt that way with him. She still felt it but had to resist the feeling.

The ease was replaced with her acting as though she didn't want to be in the same room with him. It hurt.

"Uh, thanks." He stood, taking the paper.

Ivy nodded and gave him her best professional smile. There was a flicker of something in his eyes. If she didn't know any better, she'd say he looked conflicted, or maybe hurt.

There was a knock at her office door and Deacon popped his head in.

"Hey, Ivy…oh, sorry," he said, looking at Roman. "I didn't know you had company."

"That's okay." Roman eyed Deacon with interest, standing up from the chair. "I was just leaving."

"Roman Belmonte." Deacon walked up to him and shook his hand. "How have you been, man?"

"Good," he said, shaking his hand in return. "I know how you've been, working hard for the public."

"Every day," he laughed. "I heard you'd started your own construction business?"

"You heard right." Roman nodded his head.

"That's amazing." Deacon clapped him on the back. "Do you have some business cards? I'll be glad to pass them on to people who are looking for work to be done."

"Yeah, sure," Roman said and dug some out of his pocket. "Thanks, I appreciate it."

"Yeah, no problem." Deacon smiled, his white teeth dazzling.

They all stood there for a moment, and finally Roman cleared his throat.

"Well, I'll get this sent in," Roman said to Ivy. "I'll let you know if anything changes about tomorrow."

"Thanks, Roman," Ivy said to him, watching him leave.

Deacon took a seat, leaned back, propped his feet up, and smiled up at her. He was chewing gum, his jaw clenching with each chew.

"What?" Ivy asked, crossing her arms.

"What was that?" He pointed behind him. "You guys a thing now?"

"Get your damn feet off my desk," Ivy warned.

"Yes, ma'am." He smiled and sat up straighter, dropping his feet to the floor.

"Why are you here?" she asked him.

"I'm having a party," he said.

"Okay," she replied.

"I want you to come," he told her with a laugh. "Bring Carrie and Darren. It's my birthday. I would love for you to be there. We're friends, right? That's what friends do, they go to each other's birthday parties."

Ivy looked at him for a long moment. Just then Carrie poked her head in the door.

"Did I hear party?" she asked.

"You did!" Deacon said. "At my house next Saturday. I want all of you guys to be there. It's going to be amazing!"

"Sounds good." Ivy smiled.

"Great!" He smiled too, hugging her out of the blue. "Dress up!"

"Oh, and a reason to go shopping!" Carrie clapped her hands. "Can I bring a date?"

"Sure, the more the merrier!" Deacon was in an awfully cheery mood. "See you all there!"

They both watched him leave, talking to Darren on his way out. He had obviously asked him to come too because Darren was smiling and nodding.

"Why do you look so glum?" Carrie asked. "It's just a party."

"Yeah." Ivy had promised to be his friend, but that didn't mean she trusted him. "He's just so happy. It's weird."

"It's his birthday, Ivy," Carrie laughed.

"Yeah, I need to get back to work," Ivy told her and returned to her kids.

"Miss Ivy has two boyfriends," Gemma remarked.

"I like the one in the suit," Tiffany said.

"Oh, no, the dark-haired one is way hotter," Gemma countered.

"You guys are gross," Thomas told them.

Ivy gave the girls a warning look, but Gemma and Tiffany just giggled.

The next morning, Roman and his crew were at Ivy's house. The carpet was being ripped out, and they removed the pieces of flooring that had been saturated.

The sight made her feel anxious, but she trusted Roman to do a good job. If his home was a testament to his talents, she knew she was in expert hands.

Ivy had a box of donuts that she handed to Max. He graciously took them and began handing them out to everyone.

"You didn't have to do that," Roman told her.

"I can't have you guys hungry," she said. "And I promise not to be one of those clients that hover. I'm just here to give you the carpet and tile samples I finally picked out."

"We don't care if you hover. Do we, Roman?" Max grinned and then bit into the donut in his hand.

"That's sweet," Ivy laughed. "But I have to get to work. You guys have fun."

"Thanks again for the treats." Roman smiled. "I'll see you tonight for Apollo's walk?"

Ivy nodded and walked back to her truck. She didn't realize he was still watching her until she glanced back up at the porch. He waved, and she considered not waving back, but did so anyway.

Ivy didn't want to be rude, but for her own good, she had to put some distance between herself and Roman. She thought his rejection would have weakened her feelings, but they only seemed to get stronger.

It would be much easier to avoid him once the repairs were complete and she and Apollo were back home.

Work that day was brutal. Ivy was putting out one fire after another. Her homeschool kids were wild, Darren had called out sick, Carrie was grouchy because she was overwhelmed, and a patron yelled at her for not having the new James Patterson book.

She wanted to go home, take a nice hot bath, and curl up on the couch with Apollo and a glass of wine. Unfortunately, that would not happen.

As the day was winding down and she was about to walk out the door, she got a call from the Library Director. She wanted the work-up of Ivy's proposal with Youling's estimated donation.

"I'm sorry, Ivy," Lauren sighed. "The Library Foundation asked for it and they want it tomorrow morning for their meeting."

"Do I need to be at that meeting?" she asked.

"No, they just want to see if there need to be any adjustments to their donation," she explained.

"Adjustments?" Ivy was worried.

"Don't worry." Lauren seemed to sense her discomfort. "They want to make sure that you're completely covered. They are hopeful Youling will donate the amount they are promising, but if not, they want to make preparations to help cover any costs left over. I just emailed you the spreadsheet they want you to use."

"Oh," she said, relieved. "Okay, I'll get it worked up."

"Thank you," she said.

Ivy sighed, realizing she was going to be here for at least another hour. She sent Roman a text saying she was running late, but he didn't respond. Not having time to wait on him to say anything, she got to work on the spreadsheet Lauren had sent her. It was pretty straightforward and thankfully didn't take too long to fill in, and she emailed it back to her.

Finally, she was able to leave for the night. Looking down at her phone, she realized Roman had tried to call her a few times and sent her a text asking her if she was alright. Ivy looked at her phone in confusion until she realized her text had never been sent. She would explain it once she got there.

She arrived at his house and as soon as she stepped onto the porch, the door jerked open. Roman stood there with the strangest expression on his face.

"Are you okay?" she asked him.

"Yes," he said briskly and let her inside.

"I'm sorry I'm late," she told him. "I tried to send you a text that my boss needed me to fill out a spreadsheet for the fundraiser, but it never sent. My calls and texts get dropped all the time. I really need—Roman?"

He must have been standing directly behind her because when she turned around, he was right in her face.

"I thought…I was worried," he said.

"I'm fine," she told him, concerned about how pale he looked and showed him her phone. "Look, I tried to text you."

"You don't have to prove anything to me, Ivy." He finally looked like he was regaining color in his cheeks. "I'm just glad you're okay."

Ivy felt so bad for him. He had lost a lot of people in his life and nearly lost his little brother. He must have had so many terrible thoughts when he couldn't get in touch with her. She wanted to reach out and hug him, tell him not to worry, but that would be a terrible idea.

"Where's Harper?" she asked him, trying to distract herself.

"He and Eva took Apollo for a while since you weren't here," he explained.

Ivy noticed that he hadn't moved away from her. His body was tense, staring at her in a way that made her think he might have thought he'd never see her again. She was about to say something about not stressing himself about her safety when Roman took her face in his hands and kissed her deeply.

Ivy pushed him away, keeping him at arm's length, breathing heavily.

"What the hell, Roman!" She shoved him.

"I…" he started.

Ivy turned and started for the door. Roman hurried to catch up and was on her heels.

"Wait," he said, grabbing her arm.

"You can't do that!" she said as she whirled around.

"I know," he said, but his eyes were already looking at her lips.

His hand was still on her elbow. When she didn't move, he pulled her closer, and soon she was back in his arms, his lips on hers.

She knew this was stupid. He'd said he wasn't ready. When people tell you things like that you should believe them. But his lips felt so good on hers. They felt even better as they moved down to her neck while he pulled her tighter against him. His powerful arms roamed her body, hungrily searching for something to latch on to.

When she felt his warm hands move under her coat, Ivy pulled away from him. It took every ounce of her energy to not throw herself back into his arms.

"You…can't do that," she told him, her lips throbbing from his kisses.

"I wanted to," he said.

"It doesn't matter," she told him.

"Ivy," he breathed, making his way toward her again, but she put up her hands.

"Do you want *me*, Roman, or do you want what my body can offer?" she asked him. "Because those are two different things."

He tilted his head, looking at her, not saying anything. Ivy sighed and straightened her coat and her hair.

"You don't know what you want, Roman," Ivy told him, her voice shaking with emotion. "You can't tell me you're not ready and then kiss me like that. You can't. I need space. You have to give me space."

He opened his mouth to say something, but Eva and Harper walked in with Apollo, and Roman stepped away from her. Ivy tried her best to pretend nothing had happened. She was certain Harper was clueless, but Eva looked from her to Roman with suspicion. After a few minutes of talking, Ivy thanked them for walking Apollo and then excused herself.

She had to get out of that house and away from Roman. Anger and confusion followed her into a restless sleep that night.

The next few days, she successfully avoided Roman. She thought he'd made it easier on her. He would be gone when she'd get there to take Apollo for a walk. Eva would always tell her he'd had to get to work or was working late. She seemed to want to talk to Ivy but kept her questions to herself.

On Thursday evening, he was home and greeted her at the door.

"Hey," he said as he let her inside.

"Hello." She could feel her heart swell at the sound of his voice. She had missed it.

"I've got news," he told her. "You can officially go back home tomorrow."

"Seriously?" Ivy looked up at him. "That's great!"

"Tomorrow?" Harper whined. "No! I'm going to miss seeing you and Apollo every day."

"Well, you might not see us every day, but you'll still see us," Ivy assured him.

"Yeah, and you can come to game night!" Harper said excitedly.

Ivy just smiled, feeling Roman's eyes on her. She would not give the boy false hope.

Ivy returned to her house the next afternoon. Roman said he'd meet her there with Apollo so they could do a walkthrough. Harper was there, running around the backyard. Seeing Harper playing and Roman standing on the front porch felt so right. If she were honest with herself, it was also painful. She swallowed down her emotions and walked up the porch steps.

"I hope you don't mind Harper being here," he said.

"Of course not." She smiled, watching the young boy throw Apollo the stick once more.

"So, um, I just need to do a walkthrough with you and have you sign off on everything," he explained.

"Right, lead the way," she told him.

Roman brought her inside. The smell of new wood and fresh paint greeted her. The entry and hallway had all new flooring, shiny and expertly installed. The living room had also been upgraded with new hardwood floors; a dark green area rug that matched the drapes and decor sat at its center.

"It looks amazing, Roman," she said honestly.

"Okay, let's go look at the hall bath," he said.

The wall had been completely fixed; the new toilet and sink were clean. The tile was just the right color of blue. It went well with her vintage aesthetic, especially with the big claw-foot tub gleaming white in the bathroom light.

"I have no complaints," Ivy said after Roman showed her that all the water fixtures were working.

"Okay," he said, pulling out the contract. "Just sign right here."

Ivy signed the paper and handed it back to him. They stood there for a moment, and finally Roman cleared his throat. "Well, I'll let you enjoy your evening. Bye, Ivy."

Roman moved down the hall and opened the door, calling for Harper. Soon the Belmonte brothers were down the driveway and gone. Ivy watched after them until the taillights of Roman's truck had disappeared into the darkness, knowing exactly why her heart felt a little heavier.

Chapter 10

The night of Deacon's party, Ivy and her work crew rode together. Darren drove since his SUV had more room. Sawyer and Carrie sat in the back. Ivy watched as they chatted and flirted. It was adorable. Jacob, Darren's husband, was riding shotgun, so Ivy sat in the third-row seat, which had been a task considering the dress she was wearing.

It wasn't overly short, but too short to be climbing into the very back seat of an SUV. She and Carrie had gone shopping a few days before since neither of them had anything "fancy party" appropriate. Ivy chose a red party dress that was shorter than what she was used to, and the neckline was showy, but it complimented her tall and curvy frame well. And she felt beautiful in it.

There would probably be people she knew that would judge her for it. The church ladies would clutch their pearls at the amount of cleavage she was showing. Ivy really didn't care. She wasn't wearing this dress for anyone but herself. It had taken her a long time to feel confident enough to wear something like this, and she'd be damned if anyone would make her feel bad for looking good in a pretty dress.

They arrived at Deacon's right at 7:00, and the driveway was already packed. Neatly packed, but crowded nonetheless. Deacon was extra, so he had hired a valet crew. It was probably to keep people off his immaculate lawn. It confused Ivy how the grass could look so green at the tail-end of winter.

His house sat on several pieces of cleared land, but the backyard was nearly as dense as a forest. Ivy had been here plenty of times while they were doing whatever it was they had been doing. She'd always enjoyed sitting on his back patio, watching the deer come out and nibble on fallen acorns and the squirrels jumping from branch to branch. It was a beautiful and serene property.

Right now, the two-story house looked like a frat house. People were piling inside, some were sitting out on the balcony, talking loudly and laughing, and others were hanging out on the front porch swing, drinks in hand. Granted, it looked like a well-dressed frat party considering the company that Deacon was known to keep.

The valet took Darren's SUV and parked it next to a very expensive Porsche. He and his husband looked at each other, and Ivy was sure they were wondering what they had gotten themselves into. Ivy was thinking the same thing. Sawyer and Carrie were too busy being the center of each other's attention.

When they walked into the house, they were greeted by loud music and people talking. Ivy didn't recognize anyone. Their group stuck together as they moved away from the entrance. Carrie immediately spotted Deacon and led them over.

"You made it!" he said to them. "Here, let me get your coats."

Everyone started removing their jackets, and a member of his waitstaff seemed to appear out of nowhere, taking them and giving them a number. Ivy really didn't have anywhere to put it in her dress, so Darren put it in his pocket.

"Ivy, you are stunning!" Deacon told her, kissing her cheek.

He had clearly been drinking but wasn't sloppy drunk. Ivy smiled at him and handed him a small box.

"You got me something?" He took it from her, surprised. "Thank you, Ivy!"

"It's nothing," she waved her hand. "Happy Birthday, Deacon."

Deacon opened the box and found a pair of silver cufflinks. They had an Iron Man symbol on them, embellished with red and gold.

"Are you kidding me? These are amazing!" He hugged her. "You remembered who my favorite superhero was."

"I did," she blushed. "And you said you wanted something that was 'you' when you have to be out and about. I thought this might help with that."

"You really are the best." He smiled at her.

Ivy grinned, looking down at her feet for a second. There was nothing more than friendship in her heart for Deacon, but that didn't mean she couldn't see how handsome he was. He could make anyone swoon with that smile.

"Come, let's get something to drink," he said to everyone.

"I'm the DD," Darren announced. "So, nothing for me. Do you want something, babe?"

"I can drink," Jacob said. "I'm Jacob West, by the way, Darren's husband."

"It's nice to meet you." Deacon shook his hand. "Have we met? You look familiar. Wait, are you the radio host for 98.4?"

"That would be me." Jacob smiled, his beautiful face lighting up.

If Jacob West ever needed a second job, Ivy was confident a modeling agency would hire him faster than he could blink. The saying, "he had a face for radio," didn't apply to him in the slightest. Jacob used to play football in high school and college, so he was in amazing shape. His skin was like perfectly shaped ebony, and he could give Deacon a run for his money in the smile department. He kept his dark hair closely cropped, which suited him well.

"You'll have to tell me more about that." Deacon was leading him and Darren to the minibar.

Ivy found Carrie and Sawyer looking over the vast array of food. Ivy didn't want to think about what this birthday party was costing Deacon. The food, the minibar, and the hired DJ all had to be pretty expensive. He had the money. His entire family was loaded. Ivy wondered if they were here.

She had always enjoyed talking to his mother and father. His brother was a little pompous, but sweet. Looking around, she didn't see anyone. Her heart broke for him a little. Deacon had mentioned that his parents had always been too busy for a lot of things as he was growing up. There was a fifteen-year difference between him and his brother, so they weren't exactly close.

"Here you go." Deacon handed her a drink.

"What's this?" she asked.

"Whiskey," he said, and she made a face. "I'm kidding. It's Riesling."

"It better be." She laughed and looked in the glass.

It was clear, but she still gave it a sniff. After it passed her smell check, she took a sip.

"That's good," she said. "Thank you."

"You don't trust me," he grabbed his chest. "That hurts, Ivy."

"You'll survive," she told him.

"Come dance with me," he said, grabbing her arm.

"Oh, no," she shook her head, "I haven't drunk nearly enough for public dancing."

"I'll dance!" Carrie jumped up, dragging Sawyer with her.

"Save me a dance then?" he asked, a gleam in his eyes that probably wasn't the alcohol.

"Sure," she laughed, and the rest of them made their way to the dance floor.

Ivy watched them for a little, smiling to herself, and then made her way to the food bar. She was looking over the selection when she felt a pair of arms grab her around the waist. Jumping, she spun around.

"Eva?" Ivy's heart was jumping.

"I'm so glad you're here." Eva smiled, still hugging her.

"Hey," Max said, coming up.

And then there he was. Roman stood just a few feet from her. His dark hair pushed back. He was wearing a black dress shirt and a pair of dark wash jeans. He looked 100 degrees of temptation. Ivy gulped down the rest of her wine.

"I didn't know you guys had been invited," Ivy said, hugging Eva back. "I'm so glad, too, because I don't know anyone here, and the people I do know are busy dancing."

"Me neither," Eva chuckled. "We all knew Deacon growing up, but these seem to be people he knows outside of Sparrows Ridge. I feel like a fish out of water."

"You live in New York and are on Broadway!" Ivy said to her, surprised. "Is this not the norm for you?"

"No!" Eva laughed. "I'm too busy with rehearsal. I wish I lived the NYC life people see on TV. Believe me, I love it, but I work my ass off to be show-ready. Sure, I have fun when I have time, but my work is my focus."

"I get it," she told her.

"Drinks?" Deacon had come back from the dance floor.

He brought her and Eva a glass of wine. Ivy took it gratefully and downed it just as fast as she had the first one. Roman still hadn't spoken to her, and she didn't give him the opportunity either. She walked away with Deacon as he was telling her that he had talked to Jacob about getting a radio interview for the Youling Fundraiser.

Apparently, he was going to talk to the higher-ups about getting either her or Butch on for a few questions about the expansion. He thought that maybe a little more exposure would help big investors buy up the fundraiser plates at the banquet. It was a good idea. Jacob's show broadcast all over the north half of the state. Ivy was surprised she hadn't thought about something similar.

While they were talking, Ivy watched as Taylor, from Rita's Diner, waltzed her way over to Roman. She was wearing a tight-fitting, barely there black dress. She was stunning. There was no way Roman wouldn't notice it, too. She leaned into him, saying something. He smiled and said something back, making her laugh loudly. Apparently, Roman was downright hilarious.

Ivy turned her head, feeling a certain way. She didn't want to use the word jealous. Ivy did not know what had taken place between her and Roman, but they were not together. He could flirt with anyone he wanted to, and clearly Taylor wanted to flirt with him. She grabbed another drink from a passing server as she and Deacon discussed the interview.

About an hour later, Ivy was really feeling those drinks. Carrie and Eva had convinced her to go out on the dance floor with them. She even enjoyed a few dances with Deacon. If Ivy were a bit more sober, she probably would have paid more attention to the fact that their dances were borderline inappropriate.

Ivy didn't care. Every time she looked, Taylor was practically sitting in Roman's lap. She was fueled by anger, jealousy, and wine. Not a good combination. They were awfully close on one song, their lips nearly touching. Ivy looked at Roman to see his reaction. He looked like he was ready to bruise knuckles if it came to it. Ivy smiled to herself.

Taylor came back up to him then, throwing her arms around his neck and pulling him close to her, smiling. Ivy felt the heat of anger settle in her stomach. Then she did something really stupid. She grabbed Deacon's collar, pulling him in for a kiss. A deep, let me eat your face off kind of kiss. When she came back up for air, Roman was nowhere to be seen. Ivy wasn't sure how she felt about that.

A little while later, she and the girls were getting down to T-Pain yelling, "Yeah," and some random guy had joined their trio. He was a burly man, his tie askew and undoubtedly drunk. He grabbed at Ivy, but she pushed him away.

"Come on, sweetheart," he said to her, staggering. "I've been watching you all night."

"Not interested," Ivy said to him. "Go watch someone else."

"Oh, don't be like that." He danced up to her again. "I can show you a good time."

"I was having a good time," she told him. "I don't need you for that."

"Back off, asshole," Eva said to him and grabbed Ivy around the waist.

"What, are you two lesbian lovers?" he laughed. "Mind if I join in? I'd make it worth your while."

"You're a pig!" Carrie said to him.

"Another one, the more the merrier," he laughed. "But I'll be satisfied with the blonde."

"You'd be the only one satisfied," Ivy told him, making Eva and Carrie laugh.

"You bitch," he snarled.

"No, you didn't!" Carrie yelled.

"I'm going to kick his ass!" Eva started toward him, but Ivy put up her hands.

"He's not worth it, ladies." Ivy looked him over, rolling her eyes.

"Fuck you!" he said to her.

"You wish." She winked and turned away from him.

"You don't talk to me like that." He grabbed her arm.

The next thing she knew, Roman was there. His fist went sailing past her head and made direct contact with the man's nose. Blood spurted down his face as he hit the floor like a brick.

"Roman!" she yelled as he jumped on the man as he tried to get up.

Roman punched him again. The man threw his own wild punches, but he missed terribly. Ivy saw the man's lip split as Roman landed another hit.

"Stop!" She grabbed his arm.

He turned and looked at her. His green eyes were wild, filled with rage. She pulled him to his feet and dragged him behind her. Deacon came over to check on his guest. She could hear Eva and Carrie tell him what the man had been doing. Deacon sounded pissed, but she was too worried about Roman.

She shoved him inside a bathroom and made him sit on the toilet. She ran water in the sink, splashing water on her face and the back of her neck. After she was done, she took out a washcloth and wet it in the sink. Turning to Roman, she took his hand and started cleaning it. His knuckles were bleeding.

"You're an idiot," she told him.

"Excuse me?" He looked up at her. "I was trying to—"

"I don't need you to protect me!" she snapped. "I was handling it fine on my own. Maybe if you didn't have your hand down Taylor's dress, you would have realized that."

"You want to talk about Taylor?" he laughed. "I wasn't the one sucking Deacon's face off."

"And so what if I was?" Ivy yelled at him. "He wants to kiss me! He wants me! He doesn't kiss me and then tell me he made a mistake!"

"Ivy," he said.

"Shut up!" she told him. "Just shut up!"

She grabbed his face and pressed her lips to his. It took him no time to respond. He took her hips in his hands and pulled her onto his lap. Ivy wasn't in the frame of mind for tender, sweet kisses. She was starving, hungry, and he tasted delicious.

The only thing that was going through her mind was primal, carnal desire. She was pissed at Roman, but she wanted him, every single square inch of his hard body. It didn't matter to her in that moment that he felt unable to move forward from his loss. She wasn't thinking about his heart. It was wrong, and she knew it, but she just wanted to be with him.

His tongue found its way into her mouth, sending waves of excitement through her body. She pressed herself against his groin, kissing him deeply like she needed it to survive. He moaned against her mouth, which only fueled her need.

Roman's hands grabbed her thighs. He squeezed her soft skin, working his way up her legs. Ivy shivered, as his fingers played with the hem of her panties, loving the feel of his skin on hers. But then he pulled away from her.

"You're drunk, Ivy," he told her as she continued to kiss his neck.

"And?" she whispered in his ear.

"You aren't thinking clearly," he said as her hands reached for the button of his pants.

"I don't want to think of anything right now," she told him.

"I want you, Ivy," he said, and she unclasped the button. "But I don't want you on the toilet in Deacon's house. And I don't want you drunk."

"This says differently," she teased, finally reaching what she had been looking for.

"Ivy," he seemed to growl.

There was a knock at the door, making them jump.

"Is everything okay?" Eva called.

"Yeah," Roman said, and his voice sounded shaky. "We're coming out."

Ivy looked at him and brought her hand back.

"You need to move." She stood up and jerked him out of the way.

A few seconds later she was throwing up into the toilet. Roman tried to help her, but she pushed him away. After she cleaned herself up and straightened her hair, she walked out of the bathroom without looking back at him.

She found Deacon and apologized for what had happened. He was gracious about everything. The man had been promptly kicked out. Deacon was giving her that look, the one that said he was hopeful again. She had really screwed this night up, and she wasn't sure how to fix it. It would have to wait until tomorrow. Thankfully, everyone was ready to leave, so Darren drove her home.

Ivy crashed into her bed without even taking off her shoes, praying that this was all a bad dream and when she woke up in the morning, she wouldn't have to deal with the aftermath of her drunken mistakes.

Chapter 11

There was so much that Ivy had to fix when she woke up the next day. The first thing was her massive hangover. After a very long shower and popping two Aleve, she threw on a pair of comfy jeans and her old college sweatshirt. Even though she really didn't want to, she drove to Deacon's house.

The place was quiet, and it was almost as if there hadn't been a party there the night before. She climbed the porch steps; the effort making her head pound. She would be thankful when those painkillers kicked in and did their job.

She knocked on the door a few times but got no response. Finally, she rang the doorbell and Deacon opened the door. He was shirtless, still in his pajamas, his sandy brown hair a mess on his head.

"Hey," he yawned, but smiled at her. "Come on in."

He moved out of the way and let her inside. By his expression, it surprised him that she was there. She walked around the house and saw the staff he had hired must have cleaned up as well. There wasn't a trace of trash or a speck of dust.

"What's going on, Ivy?" he asked her.

"Um, do you remember everything from last night?" she wondered, turning to look at him.

"If you're talking about you kissing me then…not if you don't want me to?" He raised his eyebrows.

"Funny," she sat down on his couch. "I shouldn't have done that."

She sounded like Roman. It was true. She felt nothing for Deacon other than friendship. If she had been sober, and she wasn't

138

trying to make Roman jealous, that would have never happened. That didn't make her feel any better.

"I didn't mind it." He smiled at her, lounging on the couch.

"Deacon—" She narrowed her eyes at him.

"What?" he said to her, laughing. "I didn't. I think Roman did, though. Is that what you were going for?"

She said nothing as she looked at him. Was it that obvious that she had feelings for him? Her cheeks went red at the thought. Who else could see it?

"Look, I'm not going to pretend like I didn't enjoy it," he shrugged. "I'm also not going to pretend like I don't want it to happen again. But I can see you're otherwise enamored with Roman Belmonte. You don't have to worry about me stepping in your way, Ivy. I just want you to be happy."

Right at that moment, Taylor came into the living room, wearing nothing but a towel.

"Oh, Ivy," she covered herself. "I didn't know you were here."

"I was just about to leave," she said.

"I'll just…go get dressed." Taylor backed out of the living room.

"Well, I can tell that you're the one that's happy." Ivy smirked at Deacon. "I'll talk to you later, Deacon."

"Ivy," he said as she headed for the door, and she turned to face him. "You're always going to be 'the one who got away.'"

Ivy gave him a small smile and left the house. Deacon would always be Deacon. It would take more of a woman than her to get him to settle down, if he ever did. She would always care for him, and she was glad they had mended their relationship, but there was no room in her heart for anyone else.

Ivy plunged headfirst into her fundraising efforts during the next couple of weeks. She hardly had time to shower, much less worry about Roman Belmonte. That didn't mean he wasn't at the back of her mind or haunting her dreams. Still, every waking moment, when she wasn't at the library, doing her day-to-day job, she was with Mrs. Forrester or Deacon.

Thankfully, Deacon seemed to be back to normal after their talk and it was mostly all business. He still flirted shamelessly, but at least she knew it was just second nature to him since he did the same thing to Elaine.

Ivy got a kick out of watching the two of them because Elaine could give it right back. She had even made Deacon blush a few times. It was truly a feat.

A week before the event, Ivy was at work, thinking about all the things she needed to do, putting away books, and came around the corner of a shelf. She stopped, and everything seemed to start spinning.

The woman stood with Carrie, her blonde hair in a ponytail, full and bright. She wore a pair of jeans, worn, but clean. Her blue sweater looked newer and had a frilly design on the front. She looked good, healthy even.

Ivy snapped to attention and raced over. The woman turned to look at her, but Ivy grabbed her by the arm and pulled her out the door before she or Carrie could say anything.

"Well, hello to you, too." The woman pulled free of Ivy's grasp.

"What the hell are you doing here, Mother?" Ivy seemed to spit the last word.

They stood in the cold, staring at one another. There wasn't much difference in appearance between them. They were both tall, fair, and curvy in the hips. Ivy's blue irises were the same shade. She was sure they could have passed for sisters if her mother had actually taken care of her body and not riddled it with drugs.

"How did you even find me?" Ivy crossed her arms, putting up an invisible shield between them.

"Facebook," she said.

"I don't have Facebook, Farrah," Ivy nearly growled.

"It wasn't your Facebook," she tried explaining. "A friend saw a news article about 30 top professionals under 30 and you were one of them."

Ivy remembered the article. The mayor had submitted her name, a reporter came, but that was it. They had sent her the magazine the article was in, but she never thought it would make the rounds on Facebook, or that her mother would run across it.

"Okay, you found me," Ivy shrugged. "What do you want?"

"Can we talk?" Farrah asked.

"We're talking now," Ivy snapped.

"I mean, can we go somewhere and talk? Like a cafe or something?" Farrah suggested.

Ivy narrowed her eyes, looking at her closely. If she were going to extend trust to anyone, the last person it would be was her mother. Still, there didn't seem to be any other way to get her away from the library. Ivy didn't want her anywhere near the things she had spent so many years building. She was toxic, and everything she touched burned.

"Let me get my things. Wait in the lobby and don't talk to anyone."

A few minutes later they were sitting in a booth at Rita's Diner. Taylor was their server and had the decency to look a little embarrassed at seeing Ivy. Ivy wanted to tell her she had nothing to be ashamed of, but it wasn't the time.

Ivy was barely sipping on the hot tea she'd ordered, all the while watching her mother, cautiously guarding her every word and movement.

The last time Ivy had seen her mother was in court. Ivy had been brought before the judge many times when it came to her mother. That time, though, she was the one in cuffs. Ivy had beaten her mother's boyfriend, Carl, and nearly broken his leg in half with a baseball bat. He had put his hands on Ivy one too many times. She'd had enough.

Her mother had shown up to the hearing in tears, claiming that Carl was a good man and Ivy a troubled young girl. Ivy still hadn't forgiven her. Actually, there were a lot of things Ivy hadn't forgiven her for and probably never would.

Something had died in Ivy that day. She wasn't sure if it were her innocence or her tolerance, maybe both. Even though she'd felt like she had lost those things a long time before, there was something about seeing her mother sitting on the opposite side of the courtroom, defending a man who had done things to Ivy that no child should ever have to endure.

She stared across the table at the woman who'd carried her, felt her grow, gave her life, and then decided she'd rather stay high than be there for her own child. Ivy had wondered so many times how her mother could leave her at the mercy of her stepfather. It had never made sense to her.

Ivy listened to her prattle on about how she'd gotten clean a year ago, about how hard it was, but not as hard as facing her demons. And on it went.

"Farrah," Ivy interrupted her. "Why are you here? Is this something in your recovery program, making amends? Because if it is, don't worry yourself about it. I moved on. I spent a lot of years putting you, Carl, and the entire ordeal behind me. So, you're off the hook. Go live your life."

Ivy could feel her face flush as rage spread throughout her body. She was angry but doing her best to keep her cool. Maybe agreeing to a chat wasn't the best idea.

"I know you hate me," Farrah said to her. "And I hear what you're saying, and yes, this is part of my recovery, but I'm here for more than that. It has taken every ounce of courage I have to come here, to face you. I don't deserve your forgiveness, so I won't ask for it. I came here to tell you I'm sorry. I'm not a fool. I know it will never make up for what I have done, but I wanted to tell you that. I'm sorry, Ivy. I am so sorry."

A tear slid down Farrah's cheek, and she brushed it away. Ivy felt her heart want to give, to soften at the sight of this weeping, broken woman. She just couldn't. She wasn't that brave. She wasn't that good.

"Are you still with him?" Ivy asked. She didn't need to elaborate. Her mother knew exactly who Ivy was referring to.

"When I got clean—" Farrah began.

"It's a yes or no question," Ivy sneered. "Are you, my mother, still with the man who beat me? The man who came into my room at night while you were passed out on the couch? The man who took away everything innocent about me? Are you still with him?"

"Ivy, you have to understand, he's changed," Farrah pleaded with her.

"I don't have to understand shit!" Ivy spat at her.

She stood up and threw money on the table. "Have a nice life, Farrah."

"Ivy, wait, please." Farrah followed her outside, the other customers watching them leave. "He's changed. I wouldn't still be with him otherwise."

"Save it!" Ivy turned on her. "I gave you enough of my time already. You said what you needed to. I'm done."

"If you would just hear him out," Farrah said to her.

"He's here?" Ivy looked around, feeling suddenly afraid, which pissed her off even more. "I can't believe this! No, actually, I can."

"It's part of his recovery, too," Farrah explained.

"Oh, that changes everything," Ivy laughed. "Let me open up old wounds so that monster can have peace! Fuck you, Farrah! Never talk to me again. Never!"

Ivy spun on her heels, tears burning for release. She saw people staring at them. It didn't surprise her. Ivy had made no attempt to control the volume of her voice. She had spent a long time and a lot of effort to keep her past and personal life off the lips of town gossipers. Now, she was sure that had all changed.

Ivy sent Carrie a message to tell her that she wouldn't be coming back that afternoon. Shortly after, Ivy pulled into her driveway. She had never been more thankful for a weekend off. Apollo seemed to know she was upset. He was extra attentive and gave more snuggles than usual when she finally settled on the couch with a hot cup of tea and a dog treat for him.

"You're the best thing to ever happen to me, bud." She scratched behind his ear.

Ivy felt so tired. Working on the fundraiser had drained her physically, and now the encounter with her mother had emotionally worn her out. It wasn't long before she drifted off to sleep during a Grey's Anatomy rerun.

Her dreams were muddled with visions that made little sense. The only thing that was clear for her was the feeling of fear. Someone was after her. They wanted to hurt her. She had to get away.

Ivy jerked awake, scaring Apollo so much he jumped off the couch. She groaned, stretching her stiff muscles. She wasn't sure how long she had slept, but her body told her it was several hours in the same position.

Rubbing her neck, she got up and let Apollo outside. He happily charged out the door and into the backyard. As she made herself a fresh cup of tea, she glanced at her phone. It was three in the morning. Ivy had slept for nearly eleven hours. No wonder her body ached.

She also noticed that Carrie had left her several texts and voice messages.

Hey, Ivy, are you alright? Who was that woman? You stormed out of here, and I'm just worried. Call me back.

I'm really worried, Ivy. Please call me.

I'm leaving with Sawyer in the morning for a weekend trip to the mountains. Can you just text me and let me know you're okay? Please?

Ivy sighed. Carrie was such a worrier, but she appreciated it. It meant she actually had people in her life who cared about her. She sent Carrie a quick text back and headed to the bathroom for a shower. After that dream, she needed to feel clean.

Ivy spent the rest of the day working on the book she planned to eventually finish. After the encounter with her mother, more material for her novel was fresh in her mind. Nothing like a little trauma to get the old writing juices flowing.

It was a memoir of sorts, but more like a journal. Thoughts and experiences from her youth were scattered throughout the pages. Mostly, it was therapeutic. Writing about it could open old wounds, but it helped to clean them out, let them heal and scab over.

The journal was one that her dad had given her on the last birthday she'd had with him. It was the last happy year of her youth. The journal was an old leather one of his that he had repurposed for her. He had made the pages himself. They were fragile, beautifully crafted, and a little withered from the years. It was perfect.

Ivy doubted she would ever submit the manuscript, but she worked on it when she could.

The writing muses were speaking to her because she realized she had worked through lunch and dinner. She was suddenly famished.

Ivy made herself a Caprese salad and a glass of wine. She sat at the table and looked down at Apollo.

"Hey, it's Valentine's Day," she told him. "Happy Lover's Day, dude."

He gave her a "gruff" in response. Ivy worked a bit more after dinner, and when she finally couldn't keep her eyes open anymore, she crawled into bed. Her prayer, as she drifted off to sleep, was that the nightmares stayed at bay.

Ivy awoke to a faint pounding noise. It took her a moment to fully come to her senses and when she did, she realized someone was knocking, pretty insistently, on her front door.

For a moment she considered going back to sleep, but she had a feeling that whoever it was had no intentions of giving up. In the next moment, she feared it was her mother. Ivy hadn't told her anything about where she lived, but this was a small town.

Groaning, and a little pissed, Ivy got out of bed and pulled on a pair of yoga pants. She threw on her college sweatshirt—that really needed to be washed—as she was making her way downstairs. She yanked open the door, ready to give her visitors a piece of her mind with some very colorful phrases.

Instead, her brain seized up as she took in Roman's tall frame and the large bouquet of flowers in his hands.

"Sorry, I didn't mean to wake you," he told her, a small smile on his lips. "Why are you sleeping in the middle of the day? Are you alright?"

"Hi, Ivy!" Harper said from beside his brother, a box of chocolates in his hands. "We came to check on you. Happy Valentine's Day, even though we're a day late."

"Check on me?" she asked as Harper handed her the box of chocolates. "Oh, thank you, Harper."

"A very concerned Carrie called me," Roman explained. "She said you had an encounter with a lady and seemed really upset. She tried to call you, but you never answered her."

"Miss Ivy," Harper said. "Um, it's cold out here."

"Oh, I'm sorry, sweetie," she moved out of their way, "Come in."

They moved into the living room, and Ivy glimpsed herself in one of the reflective surfaces of her wall decor. She looked like she'd had an encounter alright. Her hair was a mess, her sweatshirt was inside out, and there were lines of sleep on her face.

"I sent Carrie a text." Ivy took her hair down and started running her fingers through the tangles.

"I guess she didn't get it." Roman looked concerned, but also like he was trying not to laugh.

"Let me check." She ran upstairs to grab her phone.

While she was up there, she brushed her hair, her teeth, and put her shirt on the right way.

"Feel better?" Roman smirked as she came back.

"A bit," she blushed. "And I did text Carrie, but my stupid service dropped again. I just sent her another text. Crisis resolved."

"And everything's okay?" Roman asked her.

"Of course," Ivy avoided his eyes for a moment. "Why wouldn't it be?"

"Carrie said you had words with someone, a woman," Roman told her, handing her the flowers.

"Thank you," she said to him. "I'm fine, really. And you guys didn't have to do this."

"Roman said that all pretty ladies need flowers and chocolate on Valentine's Day, even if we're a day late," Harper said to her from the couch sitting next to Apollo. "And we wanted to cheer you up in case you were upset."

"Well, that's really sweet," Ivy said to him, feeling Roman's eyes on her. "But look—not upset."

Roman eyed her carefully. Ivy knew full well he didn't believe her. She hated that he was so good at reading through her bull. And if she were being honest, she liked it, too.

"What are you doing for the rest of the day?" he asked her.

"Nothing," the question caught her so off guard that she answered him honestly without having time to come up with a good lie.

"Great, Harper and I are going to make you dinner," he said.

"Oh, you don't have—" she started.

"Yes! Ivy, it will be so much fun!" Harper jumped up and ran to her. "You'll have two Valentines, even if we're a day late."

"You're not going to let that go, are you?" Roman asked him.

"Nope." He smiled.

"Well, how can I say no to that?" She narrowed her eyes at Roman, and he smiled.

This had been his plan all along. He'd brought Harper for insurance. He knew Ivy wouldn't be able to refuse him. That sly devil.

Chapter 12

When Ivy got to Roman's house, he poured her a cup of tea and led her to the couch. She tried helping him cook, but he gently and firmly kicked her out of the kitchen. She spent the time he was cooking in the other room watching TV with Harper. He was introducing her to an anime he really liked.

"So, they tried to bring their mother back from the dead, but one lost their entire body and the other one lost a few limbs?" Ivy asked him.

"Yes, you're not supposed to use alchemy to bring back someone who died," Harper said. "It's unnatural and there's a price to pay because of it."

"This is a really intense show," Ivy said, staring at the screen. "And interesting."

"Dinner is ready," Roman called to them.

They walked into the kitchen, still discussing the rules of alchemy. Roman had set the table and fixed their plates. Ivy could smell the scent of garlic and other Italian herbs.

"What's this?" Ivy asked as she sat down. "It smells amazing."

"Eggplant Rollatini," he said to Ivy's surprise. "I've never made it before, so hopefully you like it."

"Eggplant is one of my favorites." She smiled.

"Roman is the best cook!" Harper said.

"Thanks, Harp." He smiled.

They said a blessing over the food and then dug in. Ivy was surprised by how delicious her meal was. Roman had really outdone himself. She thanked him over and over as they were cleaning up.

"You don't have to keep thanking me, Ivy," he smiled. "I'm glad you're here."

They played a few board games after dinner and then retired to the living room. Harper excused himself a little while later, saying that he was too full to stay awake. They spent a few more hours catching up. Ivy told him about the fundraiser, and he told her about the new projects his business was picking up.

"That's amazing, Roman," she said. "I'm so happy for you."

"I'm really sorry about how I acted at the party," he said suddenly. "I was out of line."

"I'm the one who should apologize," she confessed, feeling embarrassed all over again. "I was drunk and made an ass of myself because..."

"Because why?" he asked, his green eyes looking from her eyes to her mouth.

"Because..." Ivy started.

Just then the front door opened. Eva and Max came in, laughing about the movie they had just seen.

"Ivy!" Eva came over, giving her a hug. "How is my favorite librarian?"

"Good," Ivy laughed. "But tired. I really need to head home."

"Do you mind keeping an eye on Harper for me while I take Ivy home?" Roman asked.

"No problem," Eva said and then winked at Roman. "Don't hurry back on our account."

Max laughed, and Roman punched him on the arm. Ivy's face turned red, and she hurried out the door, waving goodbye as she went.

As Roman was driving her home, she couldn't help but think about how she had come as a reluctant guest and now she didn't really want to leave.

"Thank you for this Roman, for inviting me over," she said to him.

"You mean forcing you to come?" he laughed.

"Well, yeah, it wasn't at gunpoint, but Harper works just as well." Ivy smiled.

"I'm glad you had a good time." He smiled back.

"Roman, I just want…" Ivy's voice trailed off as they pulled into her driveway.

A car sat there, next to her truck. Her mother got out at the approaching headlights.

"Shit," Ivy said, and as soon as the car was in park, she shot out like a bullet. "What the hell are you doing here?"

"Ivy?" Roman jogged up behind her.

"We thought you might be sleeping," her mother started.

"We?" Ivy's eyes shot to the car.

"We wanted to leave you a note." Her mother held out an envelope.

"You brought him to my home?" Ivy's voice was shaking. "How did you even know where I lived?"

"We didn't think we'd see you," Farrah said. "Please take the note."

"Ivy?" Carl got out of the car.

Ivy's entire body went stiff. She backed up instinctively, running into Roman. He placed a hand on her shoulder.

"Ivy," Carl said again. "I just wanted to say I'm sorry. I know what I did to you was wrong, but I'm a different man. And your mother, she loves you. We both do. If you could just—"

Ivy didn't remember moving. One moment she was standing next to Roman, feeling the warmth of his hand on her shoulder; the next she was on top of Carl, punching and screaming.

A few seconds later she heard her mother scream for her to stop and then felt Roman's arms around her waist, pulling her away from the flailing man.

"I'll kill you!" she screamed, fighting against Roman's hold. "Do you hear me, you sick bastard? If I ever see your face again, I'll fucking kill you!"

Her mother helped Carl into the car, his nose bleeding. One eye was already turning purple. Farrah had tears streaming down her face.

"Why?" Ivy screamed at her. "I just wanted you to love me, to choose me! But even after all these years and what he did to me, you still choose him! Why? Why? I hate you! I hate you with everything in me. I hate you!"

Farrah looked at her for a moment. She said nothing, merely got into her car and drove away.

Ivy watched the taillights fade and then crumpled. Roman caught her and carried her inside.

Apollo whined at them as Roman carried her into the kitchen, sitting her on a barstool. Her knuckles were bleeding and bruised. She had stopped yelling, but the tears continued to flow down her cheeks. Every once in a while, she would sniffle, her breath shuddering.

Roman said nothing. He asked her no questions as he found her first aid kit and began cleaning her hand. Ivy stared at the cuts, then at Roman.

"I'm sorry you had to see that," she told him. "That woman…she's my mother."

"You don't have to explain anything to me, Ivy," he told her.

"You stopped me from beating a man to death, and now you're cleaning the wounds on my hands. I owe you something," she said.

"You can tell me if you want," Roman said, as he continued to work.

So, she did. She told him about her father, his death, and how she was sent to live with her drug-addicted mother and Carl. She told him about the beatings, the violations, the neglect. When she was done, she felt raw, and the tears had returned.

"You would think I wouldn't have any more tears to cry after all these years." She wiped them away. "I wish I was stronger. I never wanted anyone to see me like this, especially not them, and definitely not you."

"Why not me?" He looked up at her as he finished putting a Band-Aid on one of her knuckles.

"I don't want you to see me so weak." She wiped another tear.

"You mean human?" Roman pointed out. "Ivy, you're one of the strongest people I know. Feeling pain doesn't make you weak. We are conditioned to keep our emotions in check, to pretend not to be human, when emotions are what make us human to begin with. There is no shame in that."

Ivy felt tears well up again, and she tried her best to push them back, despite what he had just said. As the first tear fell, Roman had her wrapped in his embrace.

"It's okay, Ives," he told her softly. "No, I guess it's not, is it? But it will be."

"Did you just call me Ives?" She looked up at him with a small laugh.

"I guess I did." He smiled.

Ivy hugged him back, clinging to him, burying her face into his broad chest. She felt it then, how in love with him she was. It terrified her, knowing that he wasn't ready to feel the same for her. She couldn't help it though. Even if it hurt her, she was going to love him.

She pulled back after a moment, and Roman kissed her forehead, then rested his head against hers. He was so close, his warm breath dancing across her face. Ivy could feel him lean into her, and she inched a little closer.

"You should go," she said, even though it pained her to say it.

"Yeah, I should," he responded, neither one of them moving.

"Roman," Ivy began. "You shouldn't kiss me. I shouldn't kiss you."

"Why?" he asked her.

"Because I want all of you, and you can't give me that." She closed her eyes, placing her hands on his face.

"I want to try," he said, and she looked at him.

"I don't know if I trust that." She shook her head.

"You can trust me, Ivy," he told her, feeling his bottom lip touch hers.

"I want to try," she echoed his words.

Roman's mouth closed around hers. It was warm and delicious and just as exciting as she remembered. His hands caressed her face as the kiss deepened. She felt bolts of electricity course through her as his lips made their way to her jawline, then her neck.

Ivy wrapped her arms around him as he leaned further into her. She felt his body tremble with excitement. Roman grabbed her waist and pulled her up, her legs wrapping around his hips.

He led her into the living room where they crashed onto the couch. Ivy lay underneath him as their mouths continued to taste and explore. Roman's hands found their way to her waist once more, slipping one hand under her shirt. As his warm fingers touched her skin, Ivy shivered.

He raised her shirt higher, kissing her stomach. Ivy's skin exploded with chills. Slowly, he unbuckled her jeans, sliding them down and tossing them onto the floor. Roman wound his fingers in the lining of her panties and slid them down, then he pulled her closer to him.

Roman kissed her thighs, working up slowly. Ivy moaned when one of his hands found her breast under her shirt. Roman's tongue suddenly found her most sensitive spot, making her breath hitch.

Ivy's back arched as he continued to work within her, grabbing fistfuls of his hair. He was gentle and slow, allowing Ivy to enjoy the feeling of his mouth on her. After a moment, he moved faster. She called out, moving against him. Roman slipped a finger inside her and then another.

"Oh, God," she cried.

Her voice, its roughness, must have filled him with need because he increased his efforts. His mouth worked harder, and his fingers moved more vigorously.

"Roman," she panted.

And then Ivy felt a sweet release, one she hadn't felt in a very long time. She moaned against the couch pillow, her body still feeling the aftershocks of pleasure. Roman moved over her, kissing her deeply.

"Take me upstairs," she commanded.

Roman lifted her and carried her to the bedroom. He laid her on the bed, and Ivy removed the rest of her clothing. It excited her to see him watch, taking in every inch of her body. She pulled Roman forward, slowly taking off his shirt and then his pants. Ivy ran her hands over his sculpted chest and down to his stomach.

They laid back on the bed, Roman over her, finding her mouth again. Ivy leaned over and handed him a condom from her nightstand drawer. After Roman slipped it on, Ivy kissed him deeply. "I want you, Roman."

Roman kissed her, both of them feeling his unspoken words of need. He pushed himself against her but stopped just before entering. Ivy smiled against his lips, relishing the tease, her desire for him intensifying.

Just when Ivy didn't think she could handle the teasing anymore, Roman gently pushed himself inside her. A million different fireworks set off inside her body. She heard him groan against her ear, sending shivers down her neck.

Roman began moving slowly, making love to her. He was gentle, but firm, pushing himself a bit further and a bit harder with each thrust. Ivy felt her body respond to him in a way that was new. No man had ever done this to her, not like this.

Ivy had already reached ecstasy tonight, but she could feel herself climbing that mountain again.

Roman sat up, pulling her up with him. Ivy moved her hips back and forth as Roman's mouth kissed one breast and then the other. He grabbed her waist, fingers digging into her skin, pulling her closer, pushing himself deeper.

His hands moved across her hips, and his fingers worked their way down to her center. Her body shook as the sensations of pleasure intensified. With him inside her and now this, Ivy was so close to the edge. She closed her eyes, feeling every ounce of indulgence rock through her.

"Look at me." His voice was rough with desire, and she opened her eyes.

Roman's green eyes were on fire. He slammed into her mouth. She kissed him hard, nibbling at his bottom lip. He stared at her again, looking deep into her eyes, using his free hand to grab her hip, holding on tight. Gratification raced through her body once more as she called out, leaning into him. A moment later, Roman followed her, his body shaking.

They held onto each other for a moment, Roman breathing heavily into her neck. Finally, they were able to move and laid back on the bed. He turned to look at her and sweetly kissed her. Ivy placed a hand on his face, caressing his cheek. There were no words for a moment like this, so no words were said. Roman wrapped her in his arms, and Ivy laid on his chest, content and happier than she had been in a long time, but afraid the moment was only fleeting.

Not wanting her anxiety to steal this moment from her, she clung to Roman, taking in his scent, the feeling of his skin on hers. She would worry about those other things in the morning. In this moment, she just wanted to be with him.

Chapter 13

They lay there for a while before Roman had to go. Ivy wanted him to stay, but she didn't voice her desires. She knew he had to get back to Harper. She watched him as he was getting dressed, admiring the taut muscles of his chest and the way his tattoos seemed alive with each movement.

"Can we talk tomorrow?" he asked her, standing by her bed, a strange look in his eye.

"Yeah," she told him, pulling the covers closer to her chest.

"See you then." He gave her a small smile and then left.

Sighing, Ivy rolled over and stared at the ceiling. So many emotions bombarded her at once. Her anger with her mother consumed her. Giving into her desires for Roman was equal parts thrilling and terrifying.

They had crossed a line there was no coming back from. Did she want to return from this new territory they were exploring? The short answer was no. What scared her was that she didn't know if he did. He had told her he wanted to try. Trying wasn't the same as yes. It wasn't the same as giving in.

At work the next day, Ivy was slammed with last-minute fundraiser preparations. Elaine had taken up residence in Ivy's office. They were poring over the guest list and entertainment schedule.

Roman had sent her a text asking if she wanted to meet for lunch. She had declined, stating she was too busy. He seemed disappointed but understood.

"Do you know who you are speaking with, young man?" Elaine was saying into her cell phone with a flurry of elegance. "I am the chairperson of the organization that is hosting this event. Yes, that's right. So, no, Mr. Forrester does not need to approve anything before you make changes. The only approval you need is mine. So, I suggest you get me the 200 salad plates—in ivory—that I need. Thank you."

Elaine hung up the phone, huffed, and mumbled something under her breath about "backwoods sexist pigs."

"I miss good old-fashioned phones on days like this," Elaine said to Ivy. "You know, the kind you can slam down after heated conversations."

Ivy laughed. Elaine got up from her seat and paced Ivy's office. She wore a pair of white slacks and a deep purple shirt that probably cost more than Ivy's entire wardrobe. Elaine had lost her shoes a few minutes after she had started working. Her bare feet were wearing a spot in the carpet.

"It helps me think," she had told Ivy when she'd seen her staring.

As the day had turned into evening, they'd finished all the tiny details that were sure to make the fundraiser a success. One of those things was the personalized invitations. Elaine told Ivy she had hosted many fundraisers, and she'd always had the best responses by doing this.

"These people have already sent in their RSVP, but this card ensures they bring their checkbooks," she said, and Ivy nodded.

She understood. Rich people enjoyed giving money after you've fluffed them up a bit. By the time Ivy was finished with her stack of invitations, her hand was numb and her stomach was grumbling.

"Excuse me, Mrs. Forrester." Elaine's assistant had accompanied her, sitting at her side, quietly helping. "It's time to leave for your dress fitting."

"Thank you, Nancy." Elaine stood up, slipping her shoes back on.

Ivy was jealous. Not that Elaine was wealthy enough for a dress fitting, but that she had a Nancy. She needed a Nancy to remind her of appointments and bring her tea. Nancy gathered Elaine's things and headed out of the office after she was instructed to start the car.

"I need a Nancy," Ivy voiced her thoughts.

"Well, you can't have mine," Elaine laughed. "I would lose my mind without that woman. She's worth her weight in gold."

"I can tell." Ivy stood as well.

"Are you alright?" Elaine asked her, taking Ivy off guard.

"Yeah, I'm fine," she told her.

"You just seem lost in thought today," she said. "Penny for your thoughts?"

"It's nothing," Ivy smiled. "I'm just excited. Eager."

"Well, it seems the only thing we have left to do is find a nice dress and you a handsome man, or woman—I don't want to assume." Elaine smiled.

Ivy laughed, slipping on her coat.

"The dress shouldn't be a problem," Ivy laughed.

"Ah, so it's the date that has you preoccupied." Elaine smiled.

"I never said that," Ivy pointed out.

"You didn't have to."

Once she was home, she saw Roman had sent her a text asking if she wanted to meet for dinner. Ivy felt her heart beat sharply. She wanted to meet him. She wanted more than that, but she didn't think it was a good idea. He was reaching out to her, but in the back of her mind she had a feeling it was because of regret.

She knew he'd said he wanted to try, but when he left her house last night, she couldn't forget that look in his eyes. The mature thing to do would be to talk about it. Ivy couldn't handle him breaking her heart right now. She told him she was tired and just needed to rest. He asked her to call him tomorrow whenever she had a moment. Ivy didn't respond.

The next day, Ivy drove to the mall because she still needed a stupid dress. She called Carrie on her way. Ivy loved shopping, but only for her vintage skirts and tops. It was an adventure, going into thrift stores and finding a plaid pencil skirt for a dollar.

Shopping for formal wear was something else entirely. Thankfully, Carrie was up for the challenge.

They met at the mall entrance and went to a few shops; Ivy tried on every dress Carrie handed her. She didn't like any of them. They just weren't her. One was too revealing, the other made her feel like she was going to prom in 1980, and the last one she tried on had a decent cut, but the color was awful.

Carrie had found hers in the first shop they'd visited. After Ivy had declined her twenty-fifth dress, Carrie called for a food break.

"I'm not trying to be difficult," Ivy said apologetically.

"I know," Carrie replied as they sat in the food court, eating Japanese takeout. "These dresses just aren't for you. I have an idea. Why don't we go to that mall-sized thrift store in Bulton's tomorrow?"

"That's like a two-hour drive," Ivy reminded her. "You want to go that far to dress shop with me?"

"Sure! Why not?" Carrie smiled at her. "It'll be a fun road trip."

They made arrangements for the next day. Ivy was excited. She loved going to Bulton's. They had all the best thrift stores.

"So, are you nervous? About the gala?" Carrie asked after a moment.

"Oh, my entire career hinges on the success of this expansion, so, no, not at all," Ivy laughed.

"Yeah, that was a dumb question," Carrie laughed with her. "Well, if anyone can pull this off, it's you, Ivy."

"That's sweet of you to say." Ivy felt herself blush a little.

"I mean it." Carrie put her fork down and looked at her friend. "When you first came to Sparrows Ridge, our poor little library was falling apart. You swooped in like Super Librarian and saved the day. You saved my job and Darren's. You helped our town in ways I don't think you even realize."

"Carrie," Ivy felt her heart swell. "Thank you. That means everything to me. And I'm glad to have you and Darren. I love this town, my job, and I love you guys with all my heart."

"I love you, too, which is why I want you to know that I am here for you if need anything or to just talk." Carrie touched Ivy's hand. "I know something happened the other day with that woman. You don't have to tell me, but I'm here to listen if you need me."

Ivy could feel tears sting her eyes. She took Carrie's hand in hers and squeezed, chokingly saying, "Thank you, Carrie. Thank you."

The next day, Ivy and Carrie spent all day in Bulton's. Surprisingly, Ivy found her dress in a matter of minutes. With so much time to spare, they hit a few other thrift stores and the local coffee shop.

Ivy found a unique mermaid lamp for her office, and Carrie bought a hat that was probably knitted by someone from the 70s. It was extremely cool and her style. Ivy found so many books for her home office and some that the library needed as replacements copies. Finding books at thrift stores was one of her favorite pastimes. They were so cheap it was criminal.

By the time Ivy was home and had unloaded her car, she was exhausted. She forced herself to shower after taking Apollo out and then crashed into her bed. As she drifted off to sleep, memories of how Roman had claimed her body went along with her. She was torturing herself.

Several more days had passed, and Ivy had made any and all excuses not to see Roman. He had asked, and she had always had something to do. She wanted to see him. Her entire body ached to pick up her phone and call him or drive to his house. What she ached for most was his body, his lips, the feel of his skin on hers.

She just couldn't do this to herself. Loving him was too painful. If she continued to give in to her feelings, knowing that he didn't return her affections, it would bury her. Roman must have realized it because for the past two days he hadn't attempted to contact her.

It was one day out until the fundraiser and Ivy was helping set things up. Elaine was also there, overseeing things, making sure that every detail down to the dinner napkins was perfect. It was nearly 10:00 PM when Elaine forced Ivy to go home. As Ivy pulled into her driveway, it shocked her to see Eva about to get into her car.

"Don't you know how to answer your damn phone?" Eva barked as Ivy got out of her truck.

"It's on silent. I was working at—" Ivy began, shocked at Eva's tone.

"Yeah, I don't care." Eva put her hands on her hips, and Ivy felt her temper flare. "I get you and my brother might not be dating, but I thought you were friends. I thought you at least cared about him, and Harper."

"What?" Ivy was confused. "Of course, I do."

"Then where the hell have you been?" Eva nearly yelled. "He's been so down. I thought he might perk up, but after the surgery—"

"Wait. Surgery?" Ivy felt her heart sink and her head spin. "What surgery? Is everyone okay?"

"He didn't tell you? Oh, he didn't, did he?" Eva huffed. "That lying… I'm so sorry, Ivy. He said he told you, and I thought you were just choosing to stay away. I was ready to tear you a new one."

"Eva, what happened?" Ivy felt fear settle in her chest.

"Everyone is fine," Eva sighed. "Roman had to have emergency surgery to get his appendix removed. He was in the hospital for a couple of days, but he's home now. And he's feeling down. I know it's because you haven't been around. What happened?"

"Nothing," Ivy lied.

"Something did." Eva searched her face. "I've never seen him like this. Look, I came over ready to throw my chancla at you, but instead let me give you some advice. Roman is a good man. He's been through a lot, but who the hell hasn't, right? It's taken him a long time to get past losing Marie, but with you…you make him happy. I see it. He cares about you, Ivy. Go see him."

With that, Eva left. Ivy stood there, unsure of what to do. It was nearly 11:00 now, but she knew she wouldn't be able to sleep tonight. She got back into her truck and drove over to Roman's house.

She wasn't thinking about how late it was or if he even wanted to see her. She just had to see his face, make sure he was alright.

He answered the door after her third knock. Roman swung the door open, looking ready to throw a few punches. His expression softened at the sight of her, but then went right back to being on guard.

"Ivy? Are you alright?" He stepped back, letting her inside.

"Me? I'm fine," she took off her coat. "Are you? Why didn't you tell me you were in the hospital? And you lied to Eva about telling me? Why?"

She couldn't keep the hurt out of her voice.

"You made it pretty clear you didn't want to talk to me." He limped slightly on his way back to the couch.

"I needed some time to process some things," she confessed as she followed him into the living room. "But having appendicitis takes precedence over things like that. Are we not friends? Are friends not there for each other when they are in need?"

"I'm fine, Ivy," he told her.

"Well, you weren't," she argued. "You were in the hospital. I could have helped with Harper or something."

"Eva and Max were here," he told her, and it felt like a slap in the face.

He didn't need her.

She felt like an idiot for driving over. Roman had been making it fine without her. What made her think that he suddenly needed her? Just because she'd fallen head over heels and it felt like she couldn't breathe when he wasn't around didn't mean he felt the same way.

"Oh, of course." She could feel tears sting her eyes. "That's great, you have them. I'm sorry. I shouldn't have barged over here so late. I was just... I'll go. Um, take care of yourself."

She turned and before she reached the door, Roman had gotten off the couch and grabbed her arm.

"Stay," he said, looking down at her. "I didn't call because I didn't think you wanted me to. And I knew you were busy with the fundraiser, so I didn't want to put more on your plate. Please, stay with me for a while."

Ivy stared into his green eyes. She saw them flicker to her mouth, making her heart skip. He wanted to kiss her, and she wanted him to. It probably wasn't the best idea. Or it could be a great one.

"I'll stay," she told him.

Roman let go of her arm and led her back into the living room. He told her about his ordeal. He had been at work when the pain started. Roman had tried to power through it, but when he realized he couldn't stand up straight, he knew he needed to go to the hospital.

"It sucked, but I'm okay now," he told Ivy. "Just a bit sore. The doctor said I can return to normal activity this weekend. I feel like I can now, but Eva won't hear of it."

"That quickly?" Ivy wondered.

"Yeah, it was a laparoscopic surgery, so not very invasive, thankfully." Roman shrugged. "It's just a bit tender."

"Well, I'm glad you're doing better," Ivy told him with a smile.

"What about you?" he asked.

"This gala fundraiser thing is going to kill me, but I'll survive," she laughed.

"You're funny, but I was talking about your mom." He eyed her, his expression serious.

"I'm doing what any mature adult would do, ignoring it by burying myself in work," Ivy tried joking.

"Ivy," Roman said, and the way he said her name made her look up.

"I don't know how I am, to be honest," she confessed, shrugging her shoulders. "I have so much going on I'm afraid if I even think about it, give her just a little bit of my time, I'll crumble. I can't afford that right now. And it's not fair. It won't be fair to let her come into my life and run a truck through it. I just can't process it all right now."

When she was finished, her hands were shaking. Roman took them in his own and pressed them to his lips. Ivy felt her heart melt a little, but fear crept into her heart.

"Don't do that." She pulled her hands away, looking down, tears in her eyes.

"What?" He looked at her, moving closer to her on the couch. "Don't do what? Don't touch you? Why? I won't. Not if you don't want me to. I just want to know what I did, Ives. Why won't you talk to me? Why have you been avoiding me? What did I do?"

"Oh my God!" she nearly yelled, bolting up from the couch, making Roman jump. "I'm in love with you, Roman. I freaking love you! Everything about you thrills me. You're the first thing I think about when I wake up, you consume my thoughts throughout the day, and you're the last thing on my mind as I fall asleep. That night I stayed over, I felt more at home than I have ever felt in my entire life. I feel at home with you and Harper. You've claimed my body, my heart, my soul, Roman. So, what did you do? You made me feel that way when you weren't ready. That's what you did to me. That's what you did!"

Ivy said all of it with tears dripping from her quivering chin. Roman sat there staring at her, shock clear on his face. Ivy thought she had broken him for a moment. He didn't even flinch, not a muscle moved. Then, Roman stood up and moved to her, his movements smooth as if one wrong step would send her fleeing.

"Please don't cry." He cupped her face with his hands, taking his thumbs, wiping away her tears. "Ivy, you have come into my life like a cleansing fire. You burned away pain I held onto for so long. I never wanted to hurt you. I never wanted to make you cry. Please forgive me. I...I love you, Ivy Newton. I knew it the moment I opened my front door and saw you standing there with Harper. The way you had your arm around him, keeping him safe from the rain. I fell hard and fast, and it scared me. I am so sorry it took me this long to be brave enough to admit it. I am ready. I am ready for you."

Roman leaned down and pressed his lips to hers, claiming her mouth with his, making sure she believed everything he had just told her. Ivy's heart flipped, sending joy through her body. Her emotions bounced from the pain of never being with Roman to the elation of having him in her arms, making her head whirl. She wrapped her arms around his neck, pulling him closer, the kiss deepening and hungry.

His hands were in her hair as he pushed her up against the wall, devouring her mouth with his own. Ivy's heart dropped, unable to deny the way his kisses took over her every thought. The way his hands on her body felt so right that it should have been wrong. She wanted all of him.

"I don't want to hurt you," she said in between his kisses. "You're still healing."

"I'm fine." His voice was deep, full of need.

Ivy let herself get lost in the feeling of his skin on hers. Too soon, he pulled away. He took her hand and led her up the stairs. They made their way into his room. Roman shut the door behind him. Ivy stood there for a moment, feeling the realization of the moment dawn on her.

They had said they loved each other. Tonight, when he took her body, it would be more than her carnal needs being met. Roman seemed to sense her timidness. He slowly walked up to her, pulling her into a soft embrace, kissing the top of her head.

"I love you," he whispered, sending chills throughout her body.

She looked up at him, thrilled at hearing those words come out of his mouth. "I love you, too, Roman."

Kissing her, he unbuttoned her shirt, letting the fabric fall to the floor. His fingers moved across her skin until he found the clasp of her bra, easily unhooking it and letting it fall next to her shirt. She shivered as he lightly moved his hands across her breasts.

Roman slid her skirt to the floor at her feet and then removed her underwear. He ran his hands up the soft skin of her legs until he felt her wetness. Ivy's breath caught in her throat as he slowly caressed her.

"It's not fair that I'm standing here naked and you're fully clothed," she told him as he continued to touch her.

"I'm enjoying the view." He smiled at her.

She grinned at him and then his mouth took over where his fingers had been. Ivy moaned with pleasure as his strong tongue worked magic within her body. She wanted him to continue, but she also wanted more. Ivy reached out and pulled his shirt over his head. She missed the touch of his mouth, but she didn't complain about seeing his bare chest. Ivy grabbed his belt and pulled him toward her, causing a fire to ignite in his eyes. He grabbed her then, kissing her passionately.

They both fell onto the bed, and Roman worked his way out of his jeans. He gripped Ivy's thighs and easily positioned himself between her legs. He gripped his hard member and slid it along her opening, her body shivering in response. After a few more passes, he thrust himself inside her, moaning as he pushed deep.

"Damn," he growled, not moving for a moment, savoring the sensation.

Then he started moving back and forth, grabbing Ivy's hips. Ivy cried out as his thrusts became harder and deeper. It was as if Roman wanted to make sure she knew he was there and never wanted her to forget it. There was no way she could, not when he was this deep inside her. It felt like pleasure and pain in the best way.

Roman leaned down, taking one of her breasts and kissing it, running his tongue across her erect nipple. Ivy leaned back, enjoying each stroke of his tongue as he explored one breast and then the other.

His thrusts were hard, rocking her entire body. She tried to keep her voice down, but it was just too much, and each time she felt him reach her spot, she called out with a deep sigh. This only seemed to encourage him because he shoved himself a little harder each time.

Ivy pushed Roman back and climbed on top of him. He gripped her hips as she rode him, calling out as he seemed to reach even deeper within her in this position. Roman lifted her hips, moving her up and down on his hard shaft. Ivy felt each movement like tiny bursts of electricity. Suddenly, her body shook with pure untamable energy as an orgasm rocked through her.

"Oh my God!" she moaned, her body clenching around him.

"Mmmm," Roman growled as he followed her just a second later, shoving himself inside her one last time.

Ivy collapsed beside him as soon as she could move. She was exhausted, but so satisfied that if the world ended in that moment, she wouldn't have cared. By the look on Roman's face, he was in the same mindset.

"Stay with me, Ives," he said, pulling her into his arms. "Stay with me tonight."

"I'll stay," she agreed.

Chapter 14

When Ivy awoke the next morning, Roman was still asleep. She watched him for a moment, his chest rising and falling, his lips slightly parted. The way his dark hair spread around his head like a mane sent tendrils of desire through her body. Instead of acting on those wants, she quietly dressed and made her way out the door.

She wasn't trying to abandon him. He needed rest, and she needed to get home. Apollo was probably pissed at her, even if he could get out the doggie door, and she had to focus on the fundraiser which was only seven hours away.

When she got through the front door, she was glad to see her dog hadn't destroyed the entire house.

"You aren't too mad at me, are you?" she asked as he licked her face when she embraced him. "I'll take that as a no. Mommy has to get a shower. I have a lot of important things to do today, so I'll be gone again tonight. I'll make it up to you later. Deal?"

Apollo licked her face again. Ivy smiled and headed up the stairs. Before she got into the shower, she sent Roman a text.

I didn't mean to disappear on you. I have to get ready for the gala.

As she turned on the water, she heard her phone ding. Ivy reached over and saw he had responded.

I figured you had to leave early to get ready for your hot date tonight.

Ivy smiled as she responded.

Unless you're meaning yourself, I don't know who you're referring to.

You want to take me to a fancy party? I don't think I'm the arm candy type.

Trust me, I'll be the envy of every lady there. That's if you're feeling up to it and can get a tux on short notice.

I think I can manage.

Meet me at my house. Elaine is sending a car.

Fancy.

For sure.

See you soon.

Ivy smiled to herself as she finally got into the shower, thankful for the piping hot water that doused her skin. Not much later she was standing in front of her full-length mirror, pulling her long blonde hair into a pretty, yet simple, updo. If she ever gave up the library gig, she might actually make a decent hairdresser.

It was a quarter past six. She hurried downstairs. Roman and the limo pulled into her driveway at the same time. Ivy patted Apollo on the head and then breezed out the door. Roman stepped out of his truck, and her breath caught. Ivy was well aware of how handsome Roman was from the moment she had laid eyes on him but seeing him in a tux was something new and exciting. He wore it well. Very well.

"You're stunning," he told her before she could say anything.

"Me?" Her eyes scanned his body.

"Yes, you, Ivy." He walked up to her, kissing her deeply.

She wanted to forget about the fundraiser, take him upstairs, and rip that tux right off him.

"I'll have to compliment you more often." He smiled at her after she released him.

"Oh, gosh," she blushed. "Please don't."

"Why not?" he asked her. "Nothing I say would be a lie."

Ivy was never vain, and it had taken her so many years to regain her self-confidence after living in a home with her mother and Carl. They had both done everything to rip her to pieces inside and out.

Still, sometimes that little voice in the back of her mind would speak, telling her she wasn't worth a second glance. It always sounded like Carl.

"If the compliment is coming from you, Roman Belmonte, I'll believe it," she told him, pushing away the old ghosts.

He kissed her again and led her to the limo. She noticed how he kept looking at her. She smiled at him. Ivy had bought this dress with no one else in mind other than herself, but she was glad he liked it.

She felt amazing in it. She loved its vintage style, but mostly because the blue velvet material brought out the blue in her eyes. It was a 1930s evening gown with flutter sleeves and hugged her around the curves of her waist. The neckline was modest, but teasing, and the back was open, nearly down to her hips.

Roman's hand touched her exposed skin as he walked her to the car.

"Thank you," she said as he opened her door.

The driver knew exactly where they were going and headed out as soon as they were settled.

"Are you feeling okay?" Ivy asked him.

"I'm fine, Ivy," he took her hand in his. "Don't worry about me all night."

"I make no promises," she laughed.

He pressed her hand to his lips, and she felt her heart do a dance. She smiled at him. She had a feeling she would do a lot of that tonight.

"I feel like I'm going to prom," Roman chuckled after a moment, looking around the limo. "This limo is nicer and there definitely wasn't champagne, though."

"I didn't go to prom," Ivy said to him, and he turned to look at her. "I've never been in a limo either."

"You didn't go to prom?" he asked, clearly surprised.

"It just didn't work out for me." She shrugged. "At seventeen, I had a full-time job. My mom and Carl spent what little they had on drugs. I had to eat and pay to keep the power on. I was too busy for prom."

"I'm sorry, Ivy," Roman said to her.

"It's alright." She looked out the car window, pretending it didn't hurt.

"It's not," he said. "Kids should be allowed to be kids."

"Well, it sounds like you had to grow up fast, too." Ivy shrugged.

"In a lot of ways, yeah," he agreed. "I still went to prom, though."

"Well, no one asked me," she shrugged again. "I didn't really talk to many people. I was going through a lot at the time."

"Hey." He nudged her. "We don't have to talk about it if you don't want to."

"It's fine." She smiled at him. "High School was just not a fun time for me, and it was mainly because of my home life. I didn't have time to think about boyfriends and prom. I didn't get picked on, not really; I just went unnoticed. I did my schoolwork, went to work, and just concentrated on getting the hell out of there."

"I understand," Roman told her. "They're still assholes for not asking you to prom."

Ivy laughed at how offended Roman was for her.

"No one wanted to go to prom with the nerdy loner chick that carried around Anne Rice and Tolkien books to read in her spare time," Ivy laughed.

"I would have," he said.

"If we had gone to school together, you would have ignored me like everyone else," she laughed again.

"There's no way I could ignore you, Ivy." He leaned over and kissed her gently on the lips.

Ivy felt that same magnetic pull in her stomach. She was happy. There were plenty of times that Ivy could have said she was truly happy and at peace. She was happy when she escaped her mother, finished her degree, bought a new house, and started her amazing job. Being with Roman was now something else she could add to that list.

The driver rolled down the partition. "We're arriving."

Ivy pulled back from Roman, but held onto his hand, loving the way his warm skin felt against his fingers.

Ivy had been working with Elaine on many aspects of the gala. When she had left the night before, there was still a lot of work to be done, so Ivy had yet to see the finished product. She was sufficiently surprised when she walked into the venue to see what the staff had accomplished.

Gold cloths covered every table. Ivory dinnerware surrounded elegant crystal centerpieces with bouquets of crimson flowers. Ivy couldn't help but notice that there were tiny gold lion emblems incorporated into the decor. Sparrows Ridge's school mascot was the lion and their colors were gold and crimson. Elaine had done her research.

"Wow," Roman said, taking in the view.

"Fancy, right?" Ivy agreed with a smile.

"And it has that Sparrows Ridge feel," he said. "You guys outdid yourselves."

"It was all Elaine," Ivy shook her head. "I just assisted."

"Don't let her fool you." Elaine came sliding up in a beautiful golden evening gown. "Ivy worked herself to the bone for this fundraiser."

"I wouldn't doubt it." Roman looked at Ivy proudly.

"Hello, Elaine." Ivy smiled. "This is Roman Belmonte."

"Belmonte…why does that sound familiar?" She shook Roman's hand.

"My cousin, Eva Belmonte, was in the Performing Arts program you funded at the high school. She's on Broadway now," Roman explained.

"Yes, Eva!" Elaine smiled. "Butch and I actually flew to New York to see one of her shows. She's extremely talented."

"Well, she wouldn't have had the opportunity without your fundraising efforts," Roman said. "I'll have to tell her I saw you. She's in town."

"Please give her my number." Elaine gave Roman a card and then turned to Ivy, putting on her business face. "Ivy, darling, our duty tonight is mingle, mingle, mingle. I want everyone to know your face, your name, your blood type if that's what it takes for them to open those deep pockets."

"Noted," Ivy laughed.

"Now, Roman," she brought her attention back to him. "You must save this old woman a dance. I would love to get to know Ivy's…"

"He's my boy—date," Ivy stumbled, feeling her face grow hot.

"Right, her date," Elaine winked. "I would like to get to know Ivy's date better."

"It would be a pleasure, Mrs. Forrester." He smiled.

"Please, call me Elaine, dear," she patted his hand. "I see guests are arriving, so let's go mingle, mingle, mingle. I must go kiss some rich ass to get money for your library. I suggest you do the same. Good luck!"

With a flurry of gold, she disappeared into the growing crowd.

"She's a firecracker." Roman said, watching her.

"Definitely," Ivy laughed. "Want to go kiss some rich ass with me?"

"Sure, girl…date." He grinned at her.

"I panicked," she shrugged. "Besides, we haven't really discussed that."

She looked down at her hands, feeling heat rise along her neck. She felt Roman's hand on her lower back as he leaned over to her.

"I'll be whatever you want me to be," he whispered in her ear.

Ivy shivered as his lips tickled her skin. She looked at him. His green eyes seemed to capture every light in the room.

"I love you, Ivy," he said to her.

"I love you, too."

He kissed her sweetly.

Ivy soon learned that neither of them were the best socializers. Roman was only slightly better than her. It wasn't until Butch swooped in to save them that they started making traction with the guests.

The man could work a crowd. Ivy was sure he'd get whatever political seat he was after.

"Well, hello, gorgeous." Deacon came up to them. "Hi to you, too, Ivy."

"You're funny," Ivy laughed as she hugged him.

"That's why you love me." Deacon smiled. "Roman, I have a question. Ivy, I hope you don't care if I steal him from you."

"As long you as you bring him back." Ivy smiled, and the two men walked away.

Ivy made her way through the crowd, saying her hellos to complete strangers, but acting like she had known them all her life. They knew her because they knew why they were there. She was the focus and center of attention. It made her nervous, and she panicked a little.

Just then she felt a warm hand on her back. She looked up and saw that Roman had returned. Her heart felt lighter, and her stomach settled.

"Are you okay?" he asked.

"I am now."

He took her hand and brought it to his lips.

"Ladies and Gentlemen," a voice came over the loudspeaker. "We welcome you to the Sparrows Ridge Library Fundraiser Gala, sponsored by Mr. and Mrs. Forrester of Somnium Charities. In ten minutes, your dinner will be served. Please take a moment to find your name card and settle in for an amazing evening. Be sure to open your hearts and your pockets."

There were chuckles all around the room.

"Tonight's fundraising goal is two million dollars," the announcer said. "We know you can help us to not only meet our goal but exceed it!"

"Ivy, Roman," Elaine came up to them. "You're sitting with us. Your staff has just arrived, Ivy. They're up here as well."

"Okay, great." They followed Elaine to their table at the front.

Ivy's face broke out into a warm smile as she saw Carrie and Darren, along with Sawyer and Jacob, sitting at the elaborately decorated table. It was nice to see familiar faces. She greeted everyone with a hug.

"You look amazing!" she said to Carrie.

"So do you!" Carrie leaned back, eyeing Ivy from head to toe. "I am so glad we drove two hours for that dress. It was so worth it. We could just auction you off and I'm sure we'd have the money in no time."

"I love the library, but not that much," Ivy laughed.

"It's nice to see you here with Roman." Carrie winked as they took their seats.

"It was a last-minute thing." Ivy blushed, not meeting Carrie's eyes.

"I'm sure," Carrie laughed.

A moment later the staff brought out their meal. Elaine explained that a Michelin Star Chef had prepared the entire menu. Ivy thought the salmon was amazing, everything tasted great, but she didn't think it was $500-a-plate amazing. And, to her, the fish at Rita's was much tastier. Though she'd never say that to a Michelin Star-winning Chef.

She could just imagine a Gordon Ramsey-like character screaming at her for her lack of culinary taste and calling her an ignorant cow.

"Ivy," Elaine brought her out of her Gordon Ramsey nightmare. "I'm headed up to the podium now to welcome everyone and then introduce you."

"Okay, sounds good." Ivy tried smiling, but she was a ball of nervous energy.

When Elaine had told her she'd be giving a speech, she had gone home and written it that night. Normally Ivy was a huge procrastinator, but she didn't want to leave this speech to chance. She'd changed a few things here and there as the weeks wore on, but one thing remained the same: she knew exactly who she was thinking about as she wrote it. Looking at Roman, her stomach settled a little. She was glad he was here.

"And now, let me introduce you to the charming and intelligent woman I have had the pleasure of working with these past few months," Elaine was saying. "Her passion and determination, and most importantly, the love of her community is why we are here tonight. Please welcome the head librarian of the Sparrows Ridge Public Library, Ms. Ivy Newton."

Ivy heard applause follow her name. Roman gave her a smile, making her heart flutter, and then she was on her feet, headed to the stage.

"Thank you," Ivy said into the microphone, her voice echoing out into the crowd. "First, I want to thank Butch and Elaine Forrester for their generosity. It may be my passion, but it's their money that made tonight possible. So, thanks for being rich."

The crowd laughed, and Butch toasted her with his glass of what she assumed was whiskey.

"And thank you, all of you, for being here tonight and giving with your heart. Elaine is right, this is a passion project. It was just a wish a year ago, but with the help of people like Sawyer Miller, who spent hundreds of hours crunching numbers, Carrie Brown and Darren West, my amazing staff, for taking up my slack when I worked on this, and Deacon Ross, who introduced me to the right people, look at where we are now."

Claps filled the banquet hall.

"Still, we didn't do all of this work for tonight," Ivy continued. "We didn't do this just so we could get dolled-up for one night and beg you lovely people for money. For us, it's about the people of Sparrows Ridge. It's about the homeschool kids who come to book club for social interaction, it's the widow who attends the knitting group so she doesn't feel so alone, it's the laid-off father of three using the library's media and education center to update his resume, it's our summer reading program that provides education, meals, and a place to beat the summer heat for over 500 children and teens. For me, personally, it's about the lives I've touched and the ones who have touched mine. It's about a young man who walked in one day to look for an Anime book and did not even realize the positive change he made in my life. He said to me one day, 'Miss Ivy, this place can never not be here. We need it.' And he's right. We do. Whatever you can do to ensure its growth, myself, that young man, my amazing staff, and the community of Sparrows Ridge will be eternally grateful."

Ivy didn't know what was happening for a moment, but she soon realized the audience was on their feet clapping. She nodded and then made her way back to her seat beside Roman.

"That was amazing," he told her, kissing her cheek.

"It was?" she asked, still shaking. "I don't even know what I said."

"All the right things!" Elaine reassured her. "With that speech, we're meeting that goal."

Chapter 15

When Ivy made it home that night, she was on top of the world. They had met their goal and more. She and Roman had danced, drank a bit too much champagne, and before she knew it, Elaine was announcing their fundraiser had been a success.

Ivy wanted to spend the rest of the night on the dance floor, but she could see that Roman was getting tired. Even though he'd said he had fully recovered from his surgery, she knew he was pushing it. After calling it a night, with a hundred promises to meet people for lunch, she and Roman were on her front porch.

He had tried to convince her, with kisses and copious amounts of naughty words, that he was fine and could stay with her that evening, but she had sent him home. She wanted him to stay. Harper was with Eva and Max so he could have, but he was in pain and she could tell.

The next morning, she woke to the buzzing of her phone. It took her a moment to realize where it was because she had just tossed it to the side once she got into her bedroom.

"Hello?" she groaned into the phone, a headache forming between her eyes.

"Miss Newton?" a man's voice, thick and weighted, asked.

"Yes?" Ivy was coming to her senses.

"Miss Newton, this is Detective Alvarez," he said, and Ivy sat up in the bed. "I'm from the San Francisco Police Department. I'm sorry to have to call you about this, but your mother, Farrah Newton, was involved in a traffic accident. Your mother passed away from the injuries she sustained. You were listed as her next of kin, her only kin, actually. I'm so sorry for your loss."

"What do I do?" Ivy felt numb.

"You'll need to come and claim her remains," Alvarez explained. "I realize you are several states away. Will she be buried here?"

"I…don't know." Ivy's fingers tingled from gripping the phone so tightly. "Did… Was there a man with her? Carl Young?"

"Yes, he has passed as well," the detective said. "I'm sorry. Was he your stepfather? I didn't see you listed as—"

"No, I just wanted to know," Ivy said. "Was…did she…was she on drugs? She was a recovering drug addict. Was anyone else involved? If so, are they okay?" Ivy could feel herself teetering on the edge of tears.

"There were no other vehicles involved," he said to Ivy's relief. "We'd had some rain, and it looks as though she hit a patch of water and slid off the embankment. There are no indications she was under any type of influence."

"I can be there tomorrow," Ivy told him.

"Yes, ma'am," he told her. "Again, I am sorry for your loss."

Ivy hung up the phone and just sat there for what seemed like hours. As if sensing her discomfort, Apollo came into the room and softly whined at her feet. Ivy finally moved, scratching his head.

"I don't know, buddy," she told him. "I just don't know."

She knew she had to move, but she felt so heavy with guilt. It wasn't because of what she had said to her mother the last time they had seen one another. It was because, deep down, she was relieved. She was relieved she would never have to see her again. That Carl could never hurt her, or anyone else, again.

There was a knock on her door. Robotically, she went down to answer it. Without even a thought to what she was wearing, or what she looked like, she opened the door.

"Hey…are you alright?" Roman asked.

"My mother died," Ivy blurted out.

"Okay," he said as he stepped inside. "How do you feel?"

"I don't know," Ivy said. "I need to go to San Francisco. Can you watch Apollo for me?"

"Yes, of course," he told her. "Do you need me to come with you?"

"No," she said. "It shouldn't take me long."

"When are you leaving?" he wondered.

"I need to book a flight." She moved to her office robotically and began pulling up flight lists.

"Ivy," Roman said a while later. "I feel like you're not really processing this."

She had booked her flight and was packing a bag. She had made a few phone calls to Darren and Carrie to take care of library matters while she was gone. Roman was taking care of Apollo, so she felt everything was covered. That was all that mattered at the moment.

"I'm fine, Roman," she told him. "I'll be okay as long as I know everything here is taken care of while I'm gone."

"Of course it will be," he told her as he kissed her on the forehead. "I'm just worried about you."

"And you're sweet to do so." They began walking down the stairs. "But I'm okay. I'll be back soon."

They walked out, and Ivy locked up. She kissed Roman and gave Apollo a big hug, and then she left.

On the flight to San Francisco, she stared out the window at the clouds. This wasn't exactly what she'd wanted to spend her savings on, and she wasn't sure why she felt obligated to do this. Had the roles been reversed, she was sure Farrah wouldn't have spent a dime on burying her.

While she had meant the last thing she had said to her mother, she couldn't help but feel a tinge of guilt eating at her. Ivy was sure that she hated Farrah; she hated the pain her mother had brought into her life. There was a time Ivy hated herself more than she could ever hate her mother, but it was only because of all the years she had allowed that hate to stop her from living.

The flight was several hours, but it wasn't long enough. The longer the flight took, the longer she could avoid seeing her mother's body. She couldn't believe she had agreed to this.

After landing, Ivy found a cab and made her way to the morgue. The morgue. Why did the name itself have to be so daunting, so cruel?

She remembered thinking the same thing when her father died. Words like, "mortuary" and "funeral home" had all left a bad taste in her mouth.

Were the words themselves imbued with some sort of mystical force of dread, or was it just because of what they were associated with?

Everything seemed to speed by like Father Time had taken a personal interest in her situation. It was all a blur. She met with a morgue employee who took her to claim her mother's body. She was sure it was her mind's way of protecting her from having to see her dead mother. Because even though her mother hadn't sustained many injuries in the crash, she still looked like a corpse.

Ivy had been to a few funerals in her life and each time she saw the makeup-covered face of a dead loved one, it didn't make her feel like they were alive. The mortician could be the best at what they did, but to her, they would always look like a dead person with makeup on. She definitely wanted to be cremated.

To her surprise, Ivy discovered that her mother had taken out a life insurance policy. It wasn't much, just enough to cover funeral expenses, but Ivy hadn't been expecting that at all. Farrah had truly tried to get her life together. Ivy hoped she had found some sort of peace while she was here. It just wasn't something Ivy wanted to be a part of.

"When would you like the viewing?" the funeral director, a plump woman in her mid-40s asked her. "We can do—"

"Mrs. Andrews," Ivy interrupted her. "I don't mean to be… There won't be a viewing, or a funeral; I just need to bury her as soon as possible."

"Oh, right, okay," Mrs. Andrews said. "Our casket options—"

"Here is a copy of her will and a copy of her life insurance policy," Ivy told her, handing her the paperwork. "Please work within those parameters. You don't need my permission for anything. Just do what she laid out."

"Of course." Mrs. Andrews seemed unfazed by Ivy's indifference.

Ivy assumed that she had been in this business long enough to see a wide range of reactions to burying a loved one.

That night Ivy found a room and ate a veggie sub while on her hotel bed. As she was eating, she got a call from the funeral home. Her mother was scheduled to be buried the following afternoon. She immediately sent Roman a message that she'd be home the next day, booked a return flight, and let the hotel know she wouldn't need the room another day. For her, it was like marking things off her to-do list.

The next day Ivy leaned her head against the cool window of the plane. For the last hour and a half, her mind had been occupied with thoughts and memories of her mother.

She had been the only person, besides the workers and minister, at her mother's burial. A few words were said and then she was laid to rest.

Before she left, the minister shook her hand and said, "I'm sorry for your loss."

Those words had been said to her so many times when she'd lost her father. Then, it had truly felt like she had lost something, a piece of her heart. With her mother, though, she felt as if she had lost her a long time ago.

When Ivy arrived home, all three of her boys were waiting on her front porch. Roman greeted her with a kiss on the cheek, and Harper gave her a big hug.

"Apollo has missed you something awful," Harper said as the big dog came up sniffing at Ivy's feet.

"Hey, big boy!" Ivy gave him a hug. "I've missed you, too."

They went inside, and it seemed like the exhaustion of the past couple of days slammed into her. All she wanted to do was fall into her bed. Instead, she made her way into the kitchen and started looking for something to eat.

"You don't want me to order something?" Roman asked.

"If I wait on food to get here, I'll fall asleep," she told him.

"You could rest, that's okay," he laughed. "I'll place an order at Rita's."

He gently took Ivy by the hand and led her to the living room. She gratefully slumped onto the couch.

"If you fall asleep, I'll wake you up when the food gets here," he told her.

"This is why I love you." Ivy curled up on the couch.

"One of many reasons, I hope." He kissed her forehead.

"I knew it!" Harper smiled, sitting on the floor with Apollo.

"You knew what?" Roman asked him.

"That you guys loved each other," he told him.

"He's a smart kid." Ivy smiled as she closed her eyes.

Ivy felt Roman trying to rouse her a while later, telling her the food had arrived, but Ivy grunted. She could hear him laugh as he picked her up and carried her upstairs.

In the middle of the night Ivy could feel Roman's body behind hers. She moved close to him, snuggling into his warmth. He wrapped his strong arms around her. After all that she had been through the past few days, having him next to her, being there, gave her a sense of peace.

Following her father's death, it had been hard for her to depend on anyone, especially in her personal life. Deacon had been wishful thinking, and there had never really been anyone serious before him. She'd had boyfriends and dated a few times, but this thing with Roman was different and special.

She nestled against him, lavishing the warmth of skin and the hardness of his chest. Roman wrapped his powerful arms around her, pulling her closer. Ivy was about to drift off to sleep again, when she felt his hand reach under her shirt and move slowly to her breast. Her breath hitched as he began to gently massage her.

Ivy laid there, allowing him to feel her, relaxing against him. He kissed her neck, holding her tighter. Tingles of desire raced down her body, settling in her stomach.

Roman's hand slid down between her legs. His rough fingers moved aside her underwear until he found her center. Ivy's body pressed against him as he began working within her.

After a moment, he took her underwear in hand, pulled them down, and pushed himself inside her, as if he couldn't control his own desire. Ivy moaned as tendrils of pleasure rocked her body. Roman grabbed her hips, pulling her closer.

He shifted her over until she was on her stomach and pulled her hips toward him. Ivy buried her face in the mattress, grabbing fists full of sheets as Roman moved behind her. She called out as he shoved himself harder against her, his fingers digging into the soft flesh of her hips.

Roman reached down and grabbed her shoulder, pulling her up until her back was against his chest. He cupped her breasts in his large hands, softly biting her neck. Holding on tightly, he continued to thrust inside her, making her moan in pleasure. Ivy turned slightly, finding his lips with her own, taking in his wet tongue.

Ivy began rubbing herself as he continued to move in and out of her, his momentum growing. She could feel the jolts of pleasure building within her. Her entire body shook, and she knew she was close to release.

"Don't stop," she said to him, and Roman gripped her tighter, pushing himself deeper. "There. Oh, God!"

Ivy's body rocked with ecstasy, the feeling so amazing and intense she nearly couldn't stand it. He held himself in place, forcing her to allow herself this feeling of complete satisfaction. Roman released himself inside her, his face buried in her neck, kissing her soft skin. He held her for a moment longer and then they collapsed on the bed, breathing heavily.

"I missed you," he said against her ear.

"I can tell," she laughed, turning to face him.

Roman kissed her deeply and pulled her against his chest. Ivy lay there, listening to his heart beat wildly against her cheek. Soon, Roman drifted off to sleep, and she followed close behind.

Chapter 16

The next morning Ivy felt heavy with sleep. All the traveling, and her tussle with Roman last night, had caught up to her. She wished she had asked off an additional day. Getting back to work wasn't something she could put off, though. Now that they had funding for the library expansion, there were mountains of work to attend to.

Roman had left earlier that morning. He'd kissed her goodbye, telling her he had to get Harper to school and go to work. She smiled, thinking about having him next to her all night. It felt good. It felt right. Knowing she couldn't wait any longer, Ivy got out of bed and took a quick shower.

As she was getting dressed, she called for Apollo. He might have already escaped out the doggy door, tired of waiting for her to let him out. She made her way downstairs, looking for him.

"Apollo, where are you?" she called as she fastened the last button of her shirt. "Come on, boy."

Ivy made her way into the living room. If Apollo didn't sleep in her bed, then she could find him curled up next to the gas fireplace. There he was, his big brown body stretched out across his plush dog bed.

"Apollo, let's go, bud," Ivy urged him.

He looked up at her, his large brown eyes closed slightly, and then he looked at her again.

Ivy's heart dropped. She knew instantly something was wrong. Rushing over to him, she gently touched his side. He whined at her.

"What's wrong, baby?" Tears sprang to her eyes. "Just hold on."

Ivy ran to her room and grabbed her phone and keys. After backing her truck up to the front porch, she put Apollo in the seat next to her as gently as she could.

On the way to the vet, she called to let them know she was coming. The entire drive Ivy kept her hand on his head, saying soothing words. She tried minding the speed limit. It's not like she wanted to hurt anyone, but she just needed to get Apollo help.

One of the vet technicians was waiting on her as she arrived. It was Rachel. She was young and had been just an intern when Ivy had first started bringing Apollo to the clinic. She and Apollo had instantly bonded. She always gave him a special treat every time he came in.

"Don't worry, Ivy," Rachel told her. "We'll get him settled. Then we'll call you back."

Rachel picked Apollo up and placed him on a cart, then wheeled him inside. Ivy followed them as far as she was allowed. For about twenty minutes she paced the lobby, sending texts to Carrie, Darren, and finally calling Roman.

"Hey," he sounded out of breath, but happy to hear from her.

"Roman," her voice cracked.

"What's wrong?" he asked.

"Apollo," she nearly whispered. "I'm at the vet. I don't know what's wrong."

"I'm on my way," he told her.

"Okay." She clutched the phone in her hands.

About thirty minutes later, Roman came sweeping into the lobby. He was dirty from the job site, but Ivy didn't care. She raced to him and allowed him to pull her into a long hug.

"Any news?" he asked.

Just then Rachel opened the door. "Ivy, you can come back."

She tried not to run as she followed Rachel. She held onto Roman's hand, Rachel leading them down the hall. It smelled like chemicals and wet fur. She watched Rachel's blonde ponytail sway back and forth like the pendulum on a grandfather clock. Tick-Tock. Tick-Tock.

"Hello, Ivy," Dr. Burton greeted her as they walked into the room. He shook her hand and then Roman's.

She immediately noticed that Apollo wasn't in there. Her heart sank.

"What's going on?" Ivy asked, wrapping her arms around her body. "Is…is it bad?"

"We've run a few tests and scans," Dr. Burton started. "Apollo seems to have a golf ball size tumor on the lower spine."

Ivy said nothing. She could hear the blood rushing in her ears like waves crashing on the shore. Her legs felt weak, but she somehow stayed on her feet.

"We don't have bloodwork back yet, but I'm not going to lie to you, Ivy. This doesn't look good," he told her. "There really isn't a best-case scenario. If the tumor is benign, we would still have to operate for Apollo to be able to walk. From what I'm looking at, even if I removed the tumor successfully, his chances of survival are slim. Based on the scans, the tumor looks to have grown around the spine."

"What…um…do you recommend?" Ivy's voice sounded hoarse. "Is he in pain?"

"No, we have him very comfortable," he reassured her. "My recommendation, surgery is too risky. It is highly likely he will die on the table. What is best for Apollo is to let him go."

"Put him to sleep," Ivy said it more to herself.

"Yes," Dr. Burton answered anyway.

"Can I see him?" Ivy asked.

"Of course," Dr. Burton told her. "Rachel, will you show Ivy to Apollo?"

"Come with me, Ivy," Rachel said gently.

Ivy followed her, Roman close at her side. She wanted to lean into him, but if she did, she knew she would crumple right there in the hallway.

They entered a small room that was dimly lit. Ivy's eyes scanned the room and landed on Apollo, his large form occupying a metal table, tubes running into his body. Her heart shattered. His dark brown eyes looked up at her. His tail wagged lightly, but he didn't move.

"I'm so sorry, buddy," Ivy whispered to him as she reached his side. "I'm so sorry. I wasn't even there the last few days."

"I…he didn't seem sick," Roman said, running his hands through his hair. "I'm so sorry."

"I've seen this before," Rachel said, trying to comfort them. "It comes on fast. There is nothing either one of you could have done."

Ivy nodded, but it didn't make her feel any better. She was sure Roman didn't feel relieved either.

She couldn't stop the guilt that was building in her chest. Instead of being with the people and her amazing dog that loved her, she had been burying a woman who had chosen drugs and an abusive man over her every time.

Ivy wasn't sure how long they sat there petting Apollo's head as Roman rubbed her back, but eventually Dr. Burton entered the room.

"I can't watch him suffer," Ivy said to the vet. "I don't want him to be in pain."

"I understand," Dr. Burton nodded his head.

Ivy watched as Dr. Burton and Rachel worked. She held Roman's hand as the two of them moved around the room for what seemed like forever. They assured her he would feel no pain and simply drift off to sleep.

Dr. Burton injected a clear fluid into Apollo's IV. She wanted to stop him, to tell him she had changed her mind. But she wouldn't do that to Apollo. She loved him enough to let him go.

The doctor and Rachel left the room to give them time. Ivy made her way back to Apollo and put her head to his. Tears pooled in her eyes, but she refused to let them fall. She had to stay strong for him. Apollo had been the one constant source of love for most of her life after the passing of her father. She could do this for him.

"What am I going to do without you?" she asked him.

Apollo's dark eyes looked at her. She could see how tired he was.

"Go to sleep, buddy," she rubbed her finger along his snout. "I'm going to miss you every day of my life, but you don't need to take care of me anymore. I'll be okay. Rest now. And thank you. Thank you for loving me. Will you do me a favor, though? Tell Daddy I said hi, and you make sure to give him a big sloppy kiss for me. Okay? I love you."

Her words seemed to be what let him finally close his eyes. After a moment, Ivy didn't hear him breathing. Tears flooded her eyes and poured down her face, dripping onto the cold tile floor.

She cried. She cried harder than she ever had in her life. Ivy wondered if there was something wrong with her. She cried tears she couldn't cry over her own mother. Roman didn't seem to know what to do, but sensed she needed a moment to herself. She was grateful for that.

She was so thankful to have him there, but she didn't want his comfort. She just wanted to feel this loss on her own. Apollo was her baby.

Rachel knocked on the door and walked in just as Ivy was wiping her tear-stained face with a tissue. She was saying something, but Ivy wasn't really understanding any of it. She nodded and signed a few things. A headache was forming in the center of her head. She just wanted to get out of there, but she wanted to take Apollo with her.

"Ivy, a lot has happened this week," Roman said to her. "I'm not saying you can't handle it. You're doing great. But if you want to go home, I'll make sure—"

"I'm fine," she told him.

"Okay." He nodded.

Ivy didn't think she was fine at all. But she had handled her father's death, her mother's, and she could handle this one. After finishing up with the vet and watching them take Apollo away for cremation, she got into her car and went home.

Roman offered to come with her, but she told him she just wanted to be alone for the night. He seemed to understand, but she could see the hurt in his eyes. He was trying to be there for her. She wanted him to be, but there was something going on inside her she had to sort out.

When she got in the house, she went straight to Apollo's bed and just stared at it. None of it seemed real. It didn't feel right she would never see him lying beside the fireplace again.

She took a seat on the couch and wrapped up in one of the many blankets she kept thrown across the back. She laid there for hours, watching the bed, imagining that at any moment Apollo would come pouncing in and settle in the thick cushion.

Ivy wasn't sure how long she laid there, but eventually she drifted off to sleep. When she awoke, it was morning. She robotically got ready for work and went in.

"Oh, honey," Carrie said to her, hugging her tightly. "I'm so sorry. About everything."

"Are you sure you want to be here today, sweets?" Darren asked her, hugging her as well.

"Yeah, I need to get to work on this expansion," she told them, not feeling at all like she wanted to do anything other than sit on her couch. "It's basically a waiting game of getting all the money cleared, but I have to help go through the proposals that are starting to pour in to actually build the darn thing. No time like the present. And it'll help keep me…occupied."

"Well, you know we're here for whatever you need," Darren said to her.

"Yes, of course we are," Carrie reassured her.

She smiled at them but couldn't find the words. She excused herself to her office and threw herself into her work. Since she was hyper-focused on the expansion, she gave Carrie and Darren a lot of her other tasks, like the book clubs and working with the local school.

For about a week, she got in early and stayed late. Roman showed up for lunch one day and forced her to eat. They chatted, but she was evasive. She knew deep down what she was doing, but it kept the pain at bay.

On Friday, she pulled into her driveway and saw that Roman and Harper were sitting on her porch.

"Hey," she said as Harper came running up to her.

Guilt hit her hard. She hadn't even seen him since Apollo had passed. Harper and Apollo had bonded so quickly. She was so consumed by her own loss that she selfishly hadn't thought about how he was handling it.

"It's so late," she told them, hugging Harper back.

"I tried calling you," Roman said. His tone was soft, but his eyes had a fire behind them. "The vet called about Apollo's ashes. They called you and couldn't reach you, so I went to pick them up."

"Oh," Ivy felt her heart drop. "I…was busy…I—where are they?"

"We made something for him," Harper told her, handing her the box in his hands. "Well, Roman did."

"I hope that's okay," Roman said.

"Yeah." Ivy made her way to the porch.

She took the box and led them inside. After taking off her coat, she opened the box. Inside was a beautiful wooden urn. It was tall and vase-like and looked to be made from a light-colored oak. Apollo's name was carved into the side.

"You made this?" Ivy looked at Roman. "When? How?"

"I started on it when we got back from the vet," he told her. "They said it would take a week to get everything processed, so I thought he could have something nice."

"Thank you, Roman," Ivy said to him.

Roman nodded. Harper sat next to her and put his head on her shoulder.

"I'm sorry, Ivy," he said to her. "I know you miss him. I do, too."

"I know you do, sweetie." She kissed the top of his head. "I'm sorry I haven't been around either. I'll do better."

"You don't need to apologize," he said. "I understand. Pain is weird. I get it. Sometimes it makes you want to hug people, and sometimes it makes you want to hide."

"You're wise beyond your years, you know that?" She smiled at him.

"That's what Roman says." He smiled back.

"Well, he's pretty smart, too," she said, looking up at him.

Roman gave them a slight smile.

Ivy placed the urn on the mantle above the fireplace, right above Apollo's favorite spot, right next to the picture of her dad. It was fitting. Ivy took a step back and gave it a sad smile. She took her place back on the couch next to Harper. He curled up next to her, and she wrapped her arms around him, enjoying the warmth of his body.

Roman finally took a seat and looked over at her. There were a million questions swimming behind those green eyes. Ivy could see all the pent-up energy, all the doubt and hurt. She looked away from him, unable to keep eye contact, knowing that the look of pain was her fault.

Harper kept them busy most of the night, but Ivy could feel the tension between them. Even through dinner, cleaning up, and sitting on the couch, Roman was there, but a million miles away. It was killing her.

"I'm tired," Harper said, yawning.

"We should get back home." Roman stood up.

"Will you please stay?" Ivy asked. She knew her eyes were pleading.

"We can't," Roman told her, and Ivy felt like her heart was going to be crushed.

"Oh, ok." She could feel her eyes sting.

"I'm going to go wait in the car," Harper said, picking up on the tension.

He gave Ivy a quick hug and left them standing there.

"Roman, I—" she started.

"I have a job out of town," he told her. "I was trying to reach you to tell you about it. You were…unavailable. I understand why, Ivy, I do, but…"

Ivy stood up and wrapped her arms around her body. Roman had more to say, but he didn't seem to know how to get the words out.

"I'll be gone for two weeks at the most," he told her.

"Does Harper need somewhere to stay?" she asked him.

"No," he said. "Eva and Max will watch him."

"Right." She nodded.

"I know you've been through so much, Ivy," he said. "And I want to be here for you if you'll let me."

"You have been," she told him. "I don't know what I would have done without you and Harper."

"Then why do I feel like you're pulling away from me?" Ivy could see the pain in his eyes.

"I'm not trying to," she said, her voice small.

"Then don't," he seemed to plead. "Just talk to me, Ives. Tell me what I can do."

"I—" She didn't know what to say.

She felt lost and ridiculous. He was going to think she was crazy.

"Has something changed?" he asked. "Do you not want this anymore?"

"No, it's not that." She looked up at him.

"Talk to me," he almost seemed to laugh. "I'm dying here."

"I'm scared to lose you," she blurted out.

"What?" He was confused.

"I'm terrified, Roman," her voice shook. "And I'm broken. My mother just died, and I haven't cried a single tear for her. And I'm okay with that. I lose Apollo and my world ends. Does that make me crazy? Do you think I'm crazy? He was everything to me. He was all I had left of my dad. I miss my dad so much, Roman; I miss him so much it hurts. I don't want to hurt anymore. I don't want to lose you or Harper. And I'm terrified that I will. I've lost everyone I have ever loved and if I lose you, I won't make it."

Roman walked up to her and took her shaking body into his arms. Tears spilled on the fabric of his shirt, but he didn't seem to mind.

"You are not crazy, Ives," he soothed her, rubbing her back with his strong hands. "Apollo wasn't just a dog. He was your family. You have every right to mourn him and to be sad."

She looked up at him, wiping her eyes. Roman kissed the top of her head.

"I wish I could take away the fear and the pain," he told her, caressing her cheek. "And I wish I could promise that one day one of us won't have to live without the other. I can't do that. What I can promise, Ivy Newton, is that I will love you every day I am on this earth. I will battle those demons of fear and pain with you. I will stand by your side and when I can't stand anymore, I will lay there with you, if you'll let me."

Ivy was speechless. She wanted to say so much, but what was there to say after that? After years of living a life of pushing people away out of anger and mistrust, here stood a man who would fight the devil himself for her. Life was pain and heartache. It could be joy and love, as well. Ivy wanted to experience all of that with Roman Belmonte.

"And I'm scared, too, Ivy," he continued. "I'm terrified; after all that I've lost, the fear that I'm going to lose you is very real. But in my heart, I know you were meant to bring Harper home that night. You were meant to heal me, make me braver, to make me a better man. And as terrified as I am to lose you, I am more scared of never being with you, of never having a life with you. So, I'm willing to conquer those fears, together, if you are."

"How do you keep making me fall more in love with you?" she asked him.

"It's a talent," he smiled down at her. "I love you, Ives."

"I love you, too, more than I can express," she said.

"Good." He leaned down and kissed her.

Chapter 17

5 years later

Ivy sat on the back patio, writing in the journal that her father had given her. It was a beautiful spring morning, the cool air rustling the leaves on the trees. She was thankful for the fire that crackled in the pit next to her chair. Laying down her pen, she picked up her tea and took a small sip, the dark brew warming her.

"Ow…" She felt a pain in her side. "Do you like the tea, too?"

Ivy rubbed her growing belly and could feel her little one move under her hand. The baby had started moving around the week before, and she was both excited and a bit overwhelmed. It was such a strange sensation.

She picked her pen up and started writing again. The journal had become more than just her experiences of pain and sorrow. There had been so much joy in her life in the past five years. The library expansion was complete, and she was able to offer so much more to her community. Max and Eva had gotten married and moved to New York. Whenever Eva wasn't busy being an amazing Broadway star, they came to visit. Or, Roman and Ivy went to see a show. Harper was about to graduate and had so many college prospects, it was like a season of the Bachelor and the universities were desperate to be given a rose.

Now, as Ivy wrote in the journal, she realized how far she had come. She put that into words. This journal wasn't just hers anymore. It belonged to Harper. And it belonged to the sweet baby growing inside her. She wanted them to know her past, and why some days she was sad, but that she still loved them.

"Hey you." Roman came out the door and walked up to her. "Are you ready to go?"

"I am, but I'm really nervous," Ivy said, closing the journal and looking up at him.

"I think that's normal." He smiled and brought her into a hug, kissing her forehead.

"I'm ready, but my bladder isn't," she laughed. "I'll meet you at the car."

A little while later Ivy and Roman met Harper in the parking lot of a faded red brick building. Harper got out of Roman's old muscle car that they had given him as a graduation present. Ivy was so surprised, Harper even more so, when Roman decided to pass it down to him. Roman loved that car, but so did Harper. About as much as he loved teasing Roman about it.

"Hey, Ives!" He hugged her. "How's my little nephew doing in there?"

"You still think the baby is a boy?" she laughed.

"Probably," he shrugged. "The Belmontes haven't had a girl since Eva, and before her birth, she was the first one in over three generations, so there is a strong possibility."

"That's what you guys keep saying." Ivy smiled. "I guess we'll find out soon enough."

"You ready to go in?" he asked her, putting his arm through hers.

"Lead the way," she said.

They walked into the large building and were greeted by the smiling receptionist. They explained why they were there, Ivy handing her the proper paperwork they had filled out the night before. She led them back to a large room, and Ivy could feel her nerves getting the best of her.

"There he is," Ivy smiled, feeling her heart flip.

He looked the same as he had in the pictures they had viewed online, chocolate brown eyes and all.

"This is Bruno," the worker told them. "I'm sure you've read all about him on our website. We don't know what he was named before he was found, but he seemed like a Bruno to us. He answers to it pretty well, but I think you can change it if you want."

"Bruno," Ivy said, and the dog's ears perked up. "You like that name, huh? I'm Ivy, this is Roman and Harper. We'd love to take you home with us if you want to go?"

Ivy crouched down, pregnant belly and all, and gently reached out to the large dog. He sniffed the air near her and moved closer. Bruno smelled her hand and then gave her a small lick. After a moment, he moved in even closer so she could scratch him behind the ear. The dog instantly slid himself against her, nuzzling her belly.

"I think he knows there's a baby in there," Harper laughed.

"Seems that way." Roman smiled as Ivy looked up at him, tears in her eyes.

"I love him," she told him.

"I know you do," he said, helping her to her feet and taking over, giving Bruno belly rubs. "I love him, too."

"I love him, three," Harper said.

"What do you say, Bruno?" Ivy asked as he began moving around them, getting pets and hugs from each of them. "Ready to go home?"

That evening, Ivy lay on the couch with Roman, Harper asleep in his recliner with Bruno across his lap. Roman had his hand on her belly, feeling their baby move. Ivy looked up at the mantle. Her dad's picture and Apollo's ashes sat there next to a family picture of her and her two boys.

It hurt looking at them sometimes, knowing that her baby would never know her dad or get to snuggle with Apollo. Other times, when she looked at the family picture, it reminded her that even though she had lost much, she had gained something amazing as well. And from that pain came perseverance and hope.

"That was a big kick," Roman laughed, feeling the baby move beneath his hand. "I never thought I would have this, Ivy. I never thought I could be this happy and at peace."

"I know what you mean." She kissed him deeply.

"Thank you," he told her.

"For what?" she wondered.

"For letting me love you," he said.

"You didn't give me much of a choice." She smiled.

"You had a choice," he said. "And you chose us."

"I'll always choose you and Harper." She leaned her head against his chest. "And the baby, and now Bruno. I'll always choose this family. I love you, Roman."

"I love you, too." He kissed her softly on her lips.

THE END

ABOUT THE AUTHOR

Amanda Guerrero-Porter is a diverse author from the deep south who enjoys weaving tales of romance that encapsulate the rich cultures that are rooted in her home state of Alabama.

Currently she's working on writing her next romance novel while also independently publishing her YA Paranormal books (under A.G. Porter). When she isn't writing, Amanda spends as much time as she can having get-togethers with her large and very loud family while they cook and play board games (aggressively).

Visit her at her website:

https://www.agporterbooks.com/romance-by-amanda-guerrero-porter

www.ingramcontent.com/pod-product-compliance
Lightning Source LLC
Chambersburg PA
CBHW031239210726
48287CB00003B/824